Ross Menshew
September 9, 2018

W9-CDH-330

Chet's Reflections

All rights reserved. No part of this book may be reproduced or transmitted in any form, or by any means, electronic or mechanical, including photocopying, recording, or by any information storage and retrieval system, without permission in writing from the publisher.

Copyright 2014 Chet and Kim Brackett
All rights reserved
Printed in the U.S.A.

Illustrated by Mike Youngman

We would like to acknowledge and thank our good friend Mike Youngman for the works of art he has created for Chet's Reflections. His love and passion for the old west is shown in detail that he carefully and masterfully weaved into each of the illustrations.   His works are inclusive of pages 3, 13,23,24,30,43,47,55,65,76,119,129,138, and of course the cover.

Thanks Mike!

Introduction to Chet's Reflections

The basis for Chet's Reflection's was a hand written journal that I found in the attic of the old rock house that I purchased in 1989. To the best of my knowledge my Uncle Chet wrote this journal in the late fifties and early sixties. He was an old bachelor who never married and he spent many a long winter evening alone with no electricity, phone or television. Writing stories of his life may have been a way to add company to those long evenings.

The rock house had been remodeled and added on to several times since my grandfather built it as a honeymoon home for my grandmother back in 1912. There had never been an upstairs to the house and no good way to put a staircase to the attic. So I cut a hole in the ceiling and added a circular stairway to get to the attic which I remodeled to make a bath and two bedrooms upstairs.

Inside the attic I found an old trunk. In it I found some family heirlooms and priceless treasures, including the journal. Parts of that journal are the writings of his book.

Since my grandparents, a series of people have lived in the house. Namely, the Patrick family. Beth and Rollie, my aunt and uncle, and then my Uncle Chet until the sixties. As he got older he gifted the place to Edna, his niece. When I bought the place it served as a home for us to stay closer to town as my high school age kids attended school.

When I found the journal, I read it and even though I couldn't believe what a treasure I had found, I put it aside as something that I would attend to when I got older and ranch affairs weren't so pressing. In 2013 we had a family reunion commemorating what would have been my father Noy's 100th birthday. I thought of the old journal and the stories that I had read. Enough time has now gone by and most of the players have passed on and promises to keep secrets have been kept.

As a history of the family, I thought it would be a good read. It helps explain some of who we are and how we got here. And just as in 1960, many of the stories were still too fresh to bring out, some parts of Chet's journal are still too fresh for me to bring out at this time. We need to remember the time, place and context in which these things happened.

One of the things that struck me the most was the importance of family.

Families are forever.

and we are a product of our families, our choices and the times in which we live.

Chet Brackett ll

This book is dedicated to those who dared to dream the dream...and worked to share them with generations, now and yet to come.

Table of Contents

Chapter 1
Bracketts to Colorado

The creaking old wagon came to a halt. Ozro pulled his team of horses up so that he could stop to read the rough map that he had carried with him since he left Wisconsin. This looked like good land he thought. There weren't as many trees but here, you could see the sky, lots of sky.

The wagon train the Bracketts had joined on this journey west had dwindled down to just a few. Most of the travelers had left the train farther north, closer to the actual town site of Denver. But with its nearly 100,000 new residents, it was just too crowded for Ozro's comfort so they just kept rolling on. They had traveled now two days south and found some land that looked to be excellent farm ground.

Ozro asked his father to come look at the land with him. Samuel, who was now 68, climbed out of his wagon and joined his son. Here lay the promise, the makings of their good new life. Trees were plentiful to the west and the foothills looked to have promising quarry loads. Father and son looked at each other and smiled in agreement. Here will be our new life, our new home.

Life in Wisconsin had been good. The Portland Quarry that they had owned was a flourishing business and the land they had invested in at Sugar Island had trees that yielded lots of maple syrup. But since Ozro's wife Harriette had died, he just didn't seem to have the passion to keep it all going. The winters were cold and seemed so lonely without her.

For the past few years, mostly to fight off his loneliness, he had taken his sons, even as young as they were, with him to gather the trees on Sugar Island. One fall and winter when Levi was four and Ira was yet two, he taught the boys to sit on the big black gelding that he used to travel between the maples to gather the syrup. Little Ira would sit, it seemed, so tall on that horse and move in rhythm with each step as the giant horse plodded along, tree to tree.

It made Ozro feel whole to see his son smile. All that fall he let the boys accompany him on the syrup trips. It even seemed as if little Ira would guide that horse with his tiny legs as they went along. Levi enjoyed the rides too, but didn't seem to relish them as much as his younger brother.

Shortly after that in the spring of 1855, Ozro met and married a beautiful young woman, Lucy Stone. She would make a good mother for the boys and a great companion for

him. Ozro now had found a new lease on life and was busy managing the quarry and the trees.

On a supply trip to Waterford, Wisconsin however they found some news that would change the course of the Brackett lives once again. While he was waiting for his supply order to be filled at the general store, Ozro's father Samuel picked up the local newspaper. It was late summer of 1858. The headlines read:

Gold Discovered!!

Gold Fever to stone masons and builders meant something different than it might mean to a wildcat miner looking for a lucky strike. The Denver area of the Kansas Territory was full of gold.

For the entire ride home after getting the supplies, Ozro and Samuel spoke of what discovering gold would mean. The influx of people, the growth of the cities, the need for builders to build the buildings. Their skills, they decided, could prove to be of great value.

Their families spent the winter preparing to leave. The quarry sold quickly and the land and maple trees at Sugar Island brought a handsome sum.

With Levi and Ira, now 6 and 8, Ozro bought an additional wagon to travel west. In this wagon would travel his building tools, extra food and a few of the household treasures that Lucy couldn't bear to leave behind. Harnessed to this wagon was the black gelding that had carried Ira on the maple runs. Confident that the boys could manage this wagon, he loaded in his own, a pregnant Lucy and placed 3 year old Alonzo Haines and 2 year old Ellen May in a fortress of bedding and quilts behind the wagon box. Ozro's parents, Samuel and Amy in the third wagon were already loaded. Their own journey here to settle in Wisconsin from Vermont years earlier classified them as trail hardy pioneers. Lucy's family came from Sauk County to bid them a tearful farewell. When they began planning this new conquest, they had been heading west to the Kansas Territory. With the gold rush and all the settlers it had now become the Colorado Territory. The land looked productive and Ozro was thrilled about the new life they were beginning.

Everyone needed to pitch in to make this Colorado grassland a home. Logs were cut from nearby timbers and corrals were built for the horses and cattle that they kept. Ira's gentle and commanding way with horses gave Ozro an idea for buying horses and taking them to the various liveries around and eventually to Denver to sell at the stockyards. His son, it seemed, possessed a natural ability to put a handle on any horse and simply convince him to do what he wanted. Maybe it was from his bonding with the black gelding at such an early age. So as the family was busy building the barns and houses to live in, Ira was given the charge of the stock...the horses mainly. He still had to help with the everyday chores, but the breaking of the colts fell to him.

The ranch the Bracketts were building on Cherry Creek, at what would soon become Franktown, was on a major route south from Denver. Many travelers discovered after two days journey, that they had a horse not quite fit to the trail. Several travelers stopped to trade a rather rank horse for one that Ira had gentled. That meant there was always some nasty bronc that needed schooling.

A while later, after they had gotten established, Ozro took the boys on a trip to Denver to sell a horse that Ira had broke to ride. As it came his turn to show his horse in the ring, the horse bucked and then he bucked some more. He made a circle twice and didn't slow a lick. Eventually Ira gathered him up and got a hold of his head. He kindly but firmly convinced him that trying to lose his rider wasn't worth it. Ira held his own, but it ended in a bust. No one wanted to buy that rotten piece of hide. That horse didn't bring a single bid. However, there was something else really interesting to come out of this attempt at a horse trade.

A man had been in the audience of buyers and walked over and introduced himself to Ozro and young Ira as a representative of the newly founded U.S. Mail delivery system called the Pony Express. He was looking for small, skinny boys under the age of 18 who could set a horse and ride him fast. He added that most generally they were looking for orphans but it wasn't a requirement. They would be interested in visiting with Ira further.

Ira's route would be about 75 miles and he would receive $25.00 per week for his pay. Ozro couldn't believe his ears. Twenty-five dollars, why that was lots of money for even men in these parts. Many a grown man could work hard all day and make only about $2.00 a day.

Ira taught his horses to do tricks that most ordinary men couldn't. One day on his mail route when he was in a stretch of known Kiowa country, he had an eerie feeling that he was being followed. Looking behind him without slowing his gait, sure enough a small band of Indians we trailing him. Just up ahead of him lay a few rolling hills and a grove of trees. He angled his path to reach those trees about the time the band caught up to him. He ducked into the forested area. When he was in far enough to feel sure they couldn't see him, he headed his horse back to the south. Here in a grassy gully he gently asked his horse to lay down. He reached up and covered the horse's eye in an effort to keep him calm as he lay quietly in the tall grass. He spoke to the beast in a soothing tone assuring him that he was alright. He could hear the Indians jabbering and yelling as they seemed to be looking for him. Finally after what seemed to be a day, the voices were gone. When he felt sure that he could get up and on his way he gigged his pony up and they resumed their route.

The pony express job only lasted a few months as the mail system adapted to new travel. However, the money that Ira earned helped to get the ranch in Colorado up and going. Ozro and Samuel with the help of the boys were building a ranch, making a water system and helping to establish Franktown.

Chapter 2
Ira; Master Horse Trainer

As Ira grew, he developed an even greater talent with horses. He and his father recognized the potential that lay ahead of him in the horse trade.

At Cherry Creek they had a small band of brood mares and a very fine stud. As the colts were born in the spring of the year, Ira would be there with them. He would play with them practically from the second that they were born. He would hold their heads in his hands and look them in the eye as if he were communicating with them telepathically. They bonded with him. But the colts weren't his only strength.

Travelers trading horses at Franktown had slowed, so Ozro would often take the boys to Denver with him and at times they would stop at the stockyards where the horse trade was being conducted. They would wait through the entire auction until the especially broncy horses were left. Ozro with Ira's advice would buy a couple of them, at a substantially reduced price. After all no man had successfully shown them or ridden them that day. Then they would head their acquisitions back to the ranch.

Ira would spend most of his days working with these purchased horses and by the time the next auction came along he would have a fine mount to show in the arena. It made him smile to know that he could work so well with the animal. It made him smile even more when that onery piece of horse hide he bought for $20.00 sold as a well-trained and mannered pleasure horse for about $65.00. They had been trading horses for several years and won more often than busted.

One of these horse trading trips in particular would shape Ira's future in a remarkable way. Ira had a horse that when he bought him had an especially hot disposition. Ira worked many hours trying to calm him. On this particular morning Ira was having a devil of a time trying to keep him traveling in the direction of Denver. Usually that 25-mile trip to the stockyards would cool most horses' blood, but not this roan that he was riding today. Truthfully, Ira was glad when they arrived and he could get off that bad cayouse. He would never let on to anyone, especially to his dad, that he was a little afraid of that horse. Somehow he felt that his ability to handle a horse was tied to his father's pride in him. As Ozro got the horses consigned it seemed that there was a lot of confusion coming from the gate near the street. A big husky man was bragging about his superior race horse and that no horse west of the Mississippi could beat him. He was even going as far as betting the flesh. The winner he said would take all. Money bet, horses ran and of course the fame.

As Ira looked longingly at the man's beautiful Tennessee sorrel stud, he thought back to the little Roan gelding that he had ridden in from Franktown. Even after 25 miles his heart was still burning, blood pumping, he wanted to go. The sorrel certainly looked built to be fast. But through his chest he was thicker and his muscles seemed looser than the Roan he had just ridden in on.

Ira listened to the big man squawk awhile then he suddenly blurted out, "Why I could go to these corrals out here and grab any old beast and I could beat you!"

Ira was almost as shocked as Ozro at the challenge that had come out of the young man's mouth. The man strutted over to Ira and looked down at him. Then he spit his tobacco, nearly in Ira's face. That act in itself washed from Ozro any feeling that perhaps his son should apologize. This big man was a bully and Ira had called him out. Ira however was grown now and old enough to make his own choices.

"You are on Sonny!!" The man half screamed, half laughed. "I'm gonna take that horse of yours," he growled at Ira. Looking at the crowd he had gathered he declared, "Tomorrow at the strike of nine we race our horses."

The crowd began to buzz. The news of a horse race seemed to attract people like flies. This rough Denver crowd loved a chance to gamble.

Ira didn't sleep well that night. He was quite sure that his Roan horse would run fast but wasn't entirely sure about keeping on top of him. In the morning out in the yards, money was being wagered. The horse betting was on. Close to nine, Ozro nodded to Ira. He made his way back to the stock pens and it seemed that all eyes were on him. Levi came to help him get his little Roan out of the corral. Ira knew that the horse would be fairly simple to catch but wanted to make a little bit of a show out of it. Horse-trading depends a lot on the show, his father had told him. He let the Roan pass by twice. The horseracing gambler started to chuckle. "This might be even easier than he had previously thought," he remarked.

Ira felt that he had made his statement. The next circle the horses made he announced that he would choose the Roan. Ira fingered his lariat and started building his loop. As the rope nestled snug on his neck, the Roan reared up. Holding the rope firmly Ira talked soothingly to the horse.

Finally somewhat in show but somewhat in actual struggling, he saddled that horse and led him down the alley and out into the street. Maybe it was Ira's imagination but this crowd was on fire. The excitement seemed to make the Roan harder for Ira to keep still. Levi came over and told him that the odds were 100 to 1.

"You can do this right?" he asked his brother with a grin on his face. Then he added, "That seems like one mean s.o.b. to me. You better beat him so we can get out of town."

Ira nervously smiled. "Hold this little sweetheart while I get on, ok. I think we may have just found his niche." Then he added, "Levi, give him an extra tug on his back cinch when I pass through the gate, It'll make for a great show." He winked at his brother. Ira swung his left leg up to the stirrup and the other over the horse in liquid motion. Then he centered his backside lightly in the saddle. It seemed as if the horse didn't even know his rider had gotten

on. The gambler's horse had a slight youth on his back but looked to be years older than Ira. The horses lined up at the starting line. The starter said, "On the count of Three."

"One."

At the count of "Two" Ira's horse whirled and ducked his head.

The starter smiled and not waiting for Ira to get his horse squared, he quickly yelled, "Three!"

He fired the gun into the air and started the race. The Roan bolted out in a huge hop and bucked about three times as Ira spurred and firmly coaxed his head in the direction he needed to go. As the horse saw an open direction and got Ira's cue which way to head he opened up the burner. The gambler's horse however had taken full advantage of the near spill and now had a significant lead. Ira again raked the steel of his spurs to the Roan's sides. That was like pouring fuel on the fire. Roanie jolted forward and Ira could feel the blood boiling in the veins of the horse beneath him. He knew his only job now was to cue this little race machine in the right direction. Now Ira loosened his already soft touch on the horse's reins. He gave him his head and just let him run. He was delighted to see how the Roan was gaining. By the time the horses reached the station where they would turn around and head back the roan was stretching his neck and sucking air even faster. Ira now was confident in how this horse would handle. He was only two lengths behind the Tennessee stud at the turn. However as they came out of the turn the Roan swapped ends much faster than his opponent. By the time the horses were half way to the finish line the Roan was pulling even. At this point Ira leaned forward on his colt's neck and began encouraging him, "Come on Roanie, you can do it, come on!" With that Ira one last time raked his steel to the Roan's sides. The Roan jumped forward and now was a half-length ahead as they crossed the finish line. Ira thought that might have been an exciting race to watch. But he didn't really even hear the cheers and even louder moans of the crowd. Ira was feeling so happy inside. This was a rush he had never felt before. "Roanie, now instead of making horseflesh cash, you'll be the star of this day's auction." Not even thinking about the race winnings, Ira was instead dreaming about what this little gold mine he was now riding was worth.

Levi was waiting for him and he grabbed the Roan's reins and pulled his brother down off the winner. He was dancing around and screaming, "We Won! We Won!"

In the middle of one of his jumps of expression, he landed hard on the foot of the already humiliated gambler who had come up behind them to speak to Ira. The gambler's words were stern and in fact more of a warning than congratulations. Even though they were seemingly disguised as such. The message was delivered..."you had better watch your backs, the both of you." A chill ran down Ira's back. "That is one mean son of a ****," he whispered.

Levi protective as always of his younger brother shrugged it off. He grabbed Ira around the neck said, "Let's go see what we won."

Ozro was already with the man who had been the purse keeper for the crowd. He looked at Ira with a huge grin on his face. "$300.00 son...THREE HUNDRED DOLLARS." He shook his head in disbelief. "I wasn't sure you were gonna make it here on that hide, let alone make a dime on him. Guess providence is smiling greatly on us today." Looking at his boys he then added, "It just keeps getting better, let's go get your new horse." Ira saw his father do sort of a jig expressing pure excitement. He smiled himself thinking about his father's excitement and just the goodness of this day.

The auction got underway and the horse-trading kicked into high gear. The Roan brought $125.00. In the flush of money, they had forgotten the harsh and chilling words of the gambler. But when the gambler's horse that Ira had won came into the ring, the boys were reminded that the gambler thought they had skinned him bad.

When that fancy blooded Tennessee stallion came into the ring there was an audible awe from the crowd. Who would have ever thought that such a grand beast would be available at a common stock sale. The man calling for the bids stopped and discussed the fineness of this horse and why he was here. Then he asked for $1000.00. Ira's jaw nearly dropped to the floor. Would they really get that kind of money for that horse? The bid caller did have to back down on his price but when he got to $800.00 the bids started flying. That fancy stud that Ira won did in fact bring the $1000.00.

That gambler and a few of his pack dog friends were standing on the other side of the auction ring. His closely set eyes seemed darker than Ira had remembered. They seemed to piece him to the core with a look of pure hate. Ira shivered. "If that guy had a gun he'd shoot us," Ira whispered to Levi.

Ozro decided that for this night, instead of rolling their bed rolls out in the livery barn the boys would be treated to a night at the Broadwell house. After all, Ira had certainly earned it. The young men had never seen such luxury. They even purchased a hot bath and a shave. Then slept on sheets that smelled of summer sunshine. The next day they purchased supplies for the ranch and then headed the wagon and the new horses they had bought south to Cherry Creek.

Chapter 3
Courting Miss Sarah

News spread fast in the now bustling town. Franktown's own Ira Brackett was a horse race master. The story was told over and over by everyone. He was fast becoming the town's celebrity. When he rode in to Franktown to deliver a horse to the livery he was surprised by the greetings that he received from all he met. He was really liking this attention, especially so when as he was leaving the livery he came face to face with the beautiful young Sarah Mauldin.

Sarah's father Miles owned a ranch not too far from their own on Cherry Creek. Ozro and Miles had been friends for several years. They had served together in the Third Colorado Cavalry.

Back in 1864 there had been some Indian raids, even in their own Franktown by the Arapahoe and Cheyenne Indians. The government had retained a large company of black servicemen from the Civil War and stationed them all around Denver. The outer towns however had to look out for themselves.

On a trip, Ozro's own family had been the victim of one such raid. Lucy and a few of the children were traveling to Elizabeth Town to help a friend who was about to deliver a child. Ozro had sent Ira and Levi to ride along beside the wagon. Knowing that this trip was only a short distance the boys took to amusing themselves along the trail.

They headed their horses after a rabbit that had hopped across the wagon's trail. With both of them chasing, the rabbit ran off farther than it might have otherwise. As he circled and darted the boys soon found themselves headed in the opposite direction of Elizabeth, and out of sight of Lucy and the wagon. They were just headed back in the direction of the wagon when they heard some blood curdling screams. They spurred their mounts. Up ahead, near a thicket of trees, a band of Indians had ambushed the wagon.

Luckily as the boys rode up, it spooked the attackers. Frightened as if they thought the cavalry was coming, the Indians left at a high rate of speed. But, as time would soon tell, not without having exacted their toll from the travelers. Lucy began to gather the kids and count heads and panic struck. Where was little Ellie? In the confusion some of the kids had bailed out of the wagon and run to the trees for protection.

They searched under the wagon in the trees and in the draw. They hadn't heard her scream. The Indians must have had her mouth covered as they rode away. By the time they had searched for the missing girl and realized that she had been kidnapped, The band was gone and no one really knew which way they had gone. Levi and Ira felt so bad. Lucy did realize that the boys riding up as they did probably saved all of their lives.

Heartbroken as she was to lose her little girls it was not Levi or Ira's fault. Finally, a few years later, she actually gave up and decided she would never see her little girl again in this life anyway.

So...when the state of Colorado called for volunteers to serve in the cavalry to control the Indian raids on the settlers, Ozro didn't think twice about signing up. He hoped that somehow he might find his little girl among those Indians.

Their regiment was only together for a short time and they did get a bad name when their colonel led them to southeastern Colorado. There they engaged in a bloody slaughter of a large band of Cheyenne and Arapahoe prisoners camped under the protection of the 1st cavalry soldiers. As their regiment came upon the Indians camp and began to attack, it became clear that these were not the warriors that they had come to fight. It was a camp of women and children. Ozro's heart raced. Hoping to find his daughter he ran through the camp yelling at the soldiers to stop. His voice however was not heard and the slaughter continued. Ozro was sickened by the carnage. He went through the camp searching among the living and the dead for his precious little girl.

Ozro's anger at the Indians, who had caused so much sorrow in his community and more personally in his own home, disappeared as he saw the inhuman treatment of the captives by his fellow soldiers.

Even after serving in the Cavalry, Ozro and Miles Mauldin remained friends. Later when Miles had lost his wife, his kids would sometimes come to stay with Lucy. Among them was a thin gangly girl by the name of Sarah who used to come out to the corrals and watch Ira as he worked the horses. She would offer to hold the reins or just to pet them. He usually told her to get lost. As Sarah grew, Miles was shot and later died. Ira began to treat her with a little more tolerance. Her uncle was now raising that family.

Even though Ira was little when his mother died, he still felt like a hole was ripped in his heart where her memory was. Sometimes Levi would tell him of a very sketchy memory he had of their mother. Ira sort of knew the pain of losing your mom but how much worse would it be to lose your father also, he thought.

Time had gone on and the Mauldin children had pretty much quit coming to the Brackett ranch. Now as a full grown woman, that Sarah...why.... she was beautiful. There were more than a few times that Ira regretted telling her to get lost. And now, she hardly even looked his way. She had all the attention of the young men in the area. At 27 years and 10 years here elder she probably thought of him more like an uncle than a beau.

And now here they were, face to face, outside the livery stable and to his disbelief, she was smiling...Smiling at him. His heart jumped in his chest, He fumbled to take his hat from his head. Holding it to his chest he slightly bowed.

"Morning Miss Sarah," he said.

She looked him up and down. She said she had been in Denver and seen his horse race show. Then she added thoughtfully, "I'm glad you beat that ole gambler."

She smiled sweetly and continued on her way. Ira stood as if frozen as she walked by. He could smell the sweetest scent of lavender and rose. Oh, she smelled good.

A couple of years ago Levi had married the beautiful and sophisticated Clara. Since that time Ira had taken to thinking more and more about taking a wife of his own. As he thought about the obvious prospects with whom he was acquainted in the area, it was Sarah who seemed to occupy his mind the most.

Ira now found himself riding his colts more often in the direction of the Mauldin's ranch. Some unseen force just seemed to pull him in that direction. One particularly chilly fall day as he was out riding, Sarah was out hanging laundry on the clothesline. When he saw her he tried to turn the colt quickly enough that she wouldn't think he was coming by to see her. He turned but was somewhat distracted by her lovely long curly hair and certainly wasn't focused on the young colt beneath him. Sensing a loosening of Ira's grip, the horse began to crow hop at first, then full out buck. Ira was grabbing leather and trying to steady his center, but it was too late. One more thrust and the colt had won. Ira landed hard on his backside on the cold ground. What a fine mess this is, he thought. I haven't been thrown in years and now it has happened right here in front of Sarah. His pride was wounded certainly. But the events of the next few moments seemed to unfold in Ira's favor. Sarah, hearing the commotion looked over her shoulder from her laundry just in time to see the colts spectacular dance. When she saw him hit the ground she ran over to see if he was ok. He had wanted to jump up and act as if the whole embarrassing incident had not happened. As she knelt close to him however, Ira decided he might like to sit there just a little bit longer. He did allow her to help him up and he leaned on her as he hobbled over to catch the colt that sullenly stood nearby.

Sarah invited him to the house. She poured for him a coffee. "Never thought I'd see a horse get the better of you." she smiled. That began a courtship that lasted through the winter and in February they were married. Ira took on more than just a wife when he took Miss Sarah's hand. She had become mother to her siblings after both of her parents had died. Ira knew that he had taken on a family.

Chapter 4

Duncans and Ketchums Come To Franktown 1884

A hot whizzing bullet cut through the leather of Tom's coat. His shoulder burned. "I'm shot, so do I die now?" He wondered. He was breathing hard and tears were stinging his eyes.

"If I cry Sam will stick the point of his boot in my back end." He tried to hold back the tears.

He spurred his horse to keep up with the others. New Mexico, he decided isn't a very friendly place. The men were moving fast, afraid that a posse might be keeping up. Tom didn't seem to get why they were so mad over a little bank robbery especially when all they stole was $2000 in gold. That sure wasn't the big haul that he had heard of from that sort of acquisition.   Tom and Sam Ketchum and their new cousins, Jim and Tap Duncan (from the marriage of their sister Nancy Blake Ketchum to Bige Duncan) had all come to New Mexico in search of work. They had heard that there was plenty, but when they arrived, it seemed that work was just day to day and it sure was hard. Even harder than when their brother Green Berry expected them to work for him.

Since Tom's father had died when he was five and then their mom a few years later, Green Berry had tried to raise his siblings and also have a life of his own. Tom and Sam just seemed to have a hard time fitting into his perception of life. So now they drifted into Folsom hot, tired and hungry. Jim ran into an acquaintance he called Lazy? or maybe it was Elzy? Tom couldn't remember. He was in town checking out a bank. The details from that point became a blur to Tom. Next thing he knew they were at the bank using their guns and asking for money. It didn't hit Tom until later that they had just robbed a bank. He had no clue at this point what he was doing but he followed the others as close and as fast as he could.

Riding out of town fast...more out of his own life's preservation than loyalty, he followed. They had ridden for a couple of hours and their horses were fully lathered and exhausted.

Tom wondered what was next. Maybe if they had a plan it would help. They slowed their exhausted horses allowing them to catch a second wind. Before long they rode upon a corral full of horses. Fresh horses.

Lazy and the Duncans quickly pulled their saddles off their spent horses and walked into the corral to catch their new rides. Sam saw Tom just sitting on his horse and told him to get some new flesh caught. Tom didn't move. He looked like the scared little brother Sam remembered after their mom died. Tom was young and Sam too but somehow, helping Tom be brave helped him feel braver too.

"I think I got shot, Sam." Tom said. Then he added that he sure wished he had one of Nancy Blake's cinnamon rolls. They were the best he ever tasted. Because Tom was the youngest he had been doted on and spoiled by his siblings. Eating sweet breads and cakes made him happy. Sam quickly looked at Tom's shoulder. He saw that the bullet had only cut through his coat. Then he was drawn immediately back to the situation at hand.

"Tom, you are ok, get your ass in gear and catch you a horse. You just robbed a bank. You need to catch a horse and get out of here. NOW! These men," Sam said pointing toward the corral, "will leave you if you slow them up."

Sam looked at Tom sternly. "Do you know what they do to men who rob banks and steal horses?" he asked.

"They dangle him by the neck at the end of a rope until they are dead." Tom grimaced and rubbed his neck. "Get up now Tom and go catch a horse."

Sam grabbed his rope and headed for the corral. Tom followed. It seemed that Sam's stern words gave him the courage needed to go on.

In the corral, Tap and Elzy had already caught their horses. Tom took a deep breath. A sleek black stud walked near him and reached his head out and sniffed Tom's hand.

"I think he likes me Sam." He smiled as he said that.

Tom caught the black horse. Sam had caught one for him and both Ketchums took their catches out to saddle up. Elzy right there announced that he was heading east and they were splitting the gold 60/40. That left $800.00 for Tom, Sam, Jim and Tap to split. More money than Tom had ever seen really. And other than the scare from the bullet and the nerve wracking run from the posse, this was not a bad way to get money. He liked it better than driving herd anyway. They took the money and opened the corral gate. They headed the horse north. The corral had held about 20 head besides the mounts they were on.

The sun had begun to set low in the sky and Jim said they would ride until it was too dark to see. Much to the four men's delight, a full Comanche moon began to rise in the night sky. It was as bright as a reading light. Sam reached into his saddle packs and pulled out a chunk of beef jerky and handed it to Tom. The new horses were fresh and made fast time until dark, but then the riders slowed to a fast trot but carefully picked their trail.

Finally about four in the morning, sleepiness began to overtake them all. There was a small box type canyon up ahead where they could corral the horses while they got just a wink of sleep. Even though it was a bit chilly, they chose not to start a camp fire just in case a posse might be following. They hadn't seen hide nor hair of the posse since the horse thief corrals where Elzy took his own trail. But just to be sure they were cautious.

They headed steadily north for several days. One morning they followed a creek down to a valley. Jim and Tap stayed near a grove of trees with the horses.

At the far end of the meadow, there were two substantial log homes and several barns and out buildings. Near what seemed to be a barn, there was a large corral. There they saw a man with a large cowboy hat working a rather wild horse. A couple of kids sat on the log fence.

About the time the riders reached the corral, the man in the hat had sent the smaller of the children to the house. He had tied the lariat attached to the wild steed to the snubbing post in one of the smaller pens. Then he walked over to the gate and nonchalantly strapped his holster to his hips. The horsemen stepped off their horses and cautiously walked over to where the man in the cowboy hat stood.

"Sam Ketchum is my name." He said. "Here with me is my brother Tom."

Ira, sensing the man's friendliness shook his hand. "Ira's mine." He replied.

Sam explained that they had come up from the south looking to sell some horses at the railhead in Denver.

Ira kept eyeing that black horse of Tom's. He reminded him so much of the gelding that Ozro had used to gather the syrup from the maples. The horse that pulled the wagon that he and Levi, only 6 and 8 years old, had driven from Wisconsin. Ira nearly teared up when he thought of that old horse. As he was growing up, next to Levi that horse was his best friend.

Sam and Tom both noticed Ira's interest in the horse. Ira asked if he had a name, Tom looked at the horse and then thoughtfully replied, "Jack. Black Jack that is."

It occurred to Sam that they could use that horse to cut a deal. The Duncans and the Ketchums needed a place to stay and get the stolen horses ready for Denver and Ira wanted that horse. Sam proposed an offer to Ira. For room and board in his barn for the next...two weeks...while they touched up their horses for Denver, the beautiful black stud would be his.

Ira wanted that black stud so he agreed. The men shook on the deal and Tom and Sam went to the tree grove on the creek to fetch Jim and Tap and the rest of the horses. When they returned Ira invited the men to join him at the house for dinner. They eagerly agreed. A good hot meal was something they had all missed for the past few months.

Ira took them to the smaller of the two log houses. He pointed to a water trough near the fenced yard where they could wash up. "My wife is kind of big on having clean hands to eat," he smiled.

He walked into the house and was warmly greeted by his lovely Sarah. Standing there in the late afternoon sun, holding their little Mary Inez, Ira couldn't have imagined a more beautiful sight. That black stud that Tom was riding hit a close second, but it was second.

Ira told her that they would have guests for dinner and actually for the next couple weeks. That wasn't a problem. Sarah never knew how many there would be at her table for a meal, so she fixed plenty. Even though Lucy did well by her kids, with 14 of them, time and all a kid wanted to eat were scarce at her house.

After dinner, Ira and his guests visited well into the night. The Duncan's spoke of the tales they had heard of the Idaho Territory. A land where the range was open and a cowboy could go for weeks viewing nothing other than his cow pony's ear, cows and his own cow camp. They said that a few years ago some ranchers had headed their herds north. They spoke of the lush grassland in the west as opposed to the Texas scrubland they were used to. Jim and Tap thought that they might sell their horses and head west. The word pictures they painted of the wild west intrigued Ira.

At some point they went out to unsaddle their horses and put their bedroll in the barn. The rest of the horse herd, they had already put in the small pasture near the corrals. At the rising of the morning sun, Lucy's big cast iron bell began to toll. Breakfast would soon be served. The outlaw crew reluctantly rose with the bell toll.

True to the deal they made earlier last evening, Tom led the black stud now called Black Jack to the large pasture that held the mares. The men stayed with Ira for nearly two weeks working the horses and getting them ready for Denver. Along with working their horses they pitched in to help with the chores around the hay ranch.

Ira and Tap seemed to share the same love of horses and for the idea of the wild open spaces of the west. Ira watched carefully the men's techniques with their horses as he tried to glean from them tips he could use in his own horse workings. He especially liked matching his own skills with those of Tap's. Sharing their skills challenged them both. Their friendship would prove to run deep.

When at last they decided the horses were ready for Denver, Ira was sad to see them go. He had so much enjoyed having these accomplished horse men in his midst. Also since they had arrived, he dreamed it seemed every night of the wide open spaces with less people where cows grazed without boundaries. He liked his new friends and he liked the sound of the Idaho Territory.

Chapter 5
We Need to Get Out of Town

Ira hadn't been to Denver to buy or trade horses in several years. In fact the last time he came up here was when the Roan had run his now famous race. Ira smiled at the thought. He had 8 fine geldings for sale and they were ready to go. On this trip he brought with him his brothers Levi and Alonzo. He needed their help in showing the horses. It was nearly evening by the time they got the horses consigned and fed for the night. The horse trading would start early the next morning.

As they drove the wagon to the livery to park it for the night, Levi looked at his bedroll. The spring weather was chilly. He commented that sleeping in his wife's warm, soft bed had made him a softer man.

"Boys," he smiled, "I am headed to the Broadwell House for dinner and a room." Alonzo eagerly joined with him. He had only been to Denver on rare occasions.

As the oldest of Lucy and Ozro's own children a lot of the responsibility of the hay ranch fell to him. A night out on Denver's boardwalk he said would suit him just fine. Ira, feigning reluctance, did in fact follow his brothers. In all truthfulness, he too, liked a soft bed to sleep in.

They checked into their rooms and Alonzo insisted that he needed a bath. After all he didn't have a wife yet to make him clean up as much as the other two. He even had a shave. As they wandered downstairs to eat dinner, they could hear a tinny piano playing one of their favorite songs. They skipped the dinner table and wandered out on the boardwalk. Alonzo found the swinging doors of a saloon and before Ira could object, they had walked into the hall where the piano played.

As they stood just inside the bar, Ira's blood ran chill. There at the poker table, staring at him was the gambler...the one who the Roan had beaten in the horse race. They hadn't exactly parted with words of friendship the last time that Ira saw him. Ira tried not to look at him and was silently hoping maybe he would not remember him.

The brothers walked to the bar and ordered a bottle of whiskey. Each poured a glass and stared at the mirrored wall that made the backdrop behind the bar. The gambler cleared his throat and folded his hand. "Weren't good cards anyways." He muttered.

"Barkeep!" He growled. "What do you mean serving such a little feller, why he gotta still be a boy as short as he is."

A few people in the saloon laughed. Some left knowing a fight was brewing. Ira started to turn and look at the gambler but Levi grabbed the back of his neck hard and whispered sternly.

"Keep your eyes up here," he nodded toward the mirror. The gambler walked over and stood close behind Ira.

"Didn't ya hear me Shorty?" he asked.

At this point Levi slid off his stool and stood between Ira's back and the big man.

"Why don't you just go back to your business, mister and we'll just mind ours," Levi suggested.

Even though Levi was taller than Ira, he was somewhat thin and only about half the width of the gambler. He looked at Levi and smiled then spat his tobacco on Levi's boot. Those were the nicest pair of boots Levi had ever owned and he was really proud of them.

"We had better get outta here." Ira whispered to Alonzo.

Just then Alonzo shifted on his stool and the gambler must have thought he was making his move. A heavy left fist from that big man sent Levi scrambling to the floor. Now with Levi out of the way he grabbed Ira from behind. Ira grabbed the half full whiskey bottle and slammed it hard to the man's head. As that gambler fell to his knees several more men joined in and Ira heard the gambler cussing "those filthy Brackett boys" and detailing all the things he was gonna do to them and their families if he ever caught them in his territory again. Even though Alonzo got a few good licks in he took his share. The saloonkeeper, finally fed up with this behavior, pulled out his buck shot gun and fired it twice in the air.

"The sheriff's on his way," he yelled in a very commanding voice, "and I suggest you all should be too!"

The brothers half left, half were escorted out of the saloon. They felt a bit uneasy as they passed the dark alleyway on the way back to the boarding house. They weren't sure where the gambler and his compadres were. They were relieved when they arrived safely back at the big house.

No one however slept well that night. Ira thought maybe he had a broken rib and both of Alonzo's eyes would probably be swollen shut.

"Would anyone buy a horse ridden by a man who obviously was beaten up in a barroom brawl?" Ira muttered to himself.

At the crack of dawn, Ira went out to the livery to get extra halters for the horses in the yards from the wagon. Opening the livery doors, he was stunned and sickened by what he saw. The sorrel gelding that pulled his light wagon lay on the floor in a pool of blood. Somewhere in the night, someone had shot him and slit his throat.

Ira remembered the things that the gambler had said he would do to him and his wife and family if he ever caught him in his territory again. Idle threats they weren't. That gambler knew Sarah. He was a friend to her uncle. He was always trying to hit on Sarah. One time when they were here in Denver a street dance was going on. That man asked her to dance. Because she was young and because she wanted to dance she said yes. He tried to kiss her and Sarah slapped him hard. Then her uncle beat her for that. "That gambler helps put food on our table," He said.

So not only had Ira wounded this man's pride at the horse race, won his fancy horse, engaged in a nasty bar fight, but Ira's wife had turned him down too. Nearly comical Ira thought, but then as he stood looking at his dead horse there in that pool of blood...it didn't seem funny at all.

Ira pulled his hat off and rubbed his head as if to force some thoughts straight into his brain. He wondered if they should even stay to finish their horse business. Leaving the halters he went back to find his brothers. He was getting more apprehensive as time wore on. Visiting with Levi and Alonzo, they decided to stay until they sold the horses and then high tail it out of town. They kept back one of the geldings to pull the wagon.

On the way home Ira began to visit with Levi about the Idaho Territory. He told him of all the tales the Ketchums and Duncans had painted about where the grass, stirrup high to a horse, was free for the taking.

Levi wasn't falling for the beauty of it all. "What could be more beautiful than my Clara and the ranch my father-in-law needs me to help him run?" He looked at Ira and said, "We are just beginning to grow a family and prosper."

As for Alonzo, well he was busy trying to keep his swollen eyes shut and his head from hurting. So Ira quit trying to recruit Levi. He could clearly see how good Levi's life here was. Truthfully, it was with Ira that the gambler had a problem. So if it weren't for Ira's horse trading bringing them to Denver maybe the rest of them could stay out of the gamblers way.

Ira began to quietly add up in his mind what money he had and what he and Sarah could sell. He felt surer with each clop of the horses hooves that he needed to get out of town, and fast. He started to share the profit he made on the geldings with Levi when they stopped to drop him off at the Crowfoot's ranch. Levi looked at the dollars that Ira had placed in his hand. He handed them back to his brother.

"I can tell that you've got it determined in your mind to leave for the Idaho. I wish you'd change your mind".He paused. "But if you are going you are surely gonna need this and some more." He paused again, "If I can help you Ira, let me know."

Alonzo was worried about what he would face when he returned home. Ira told him that he would help explain it to their father. When Ira finally pulled the wagon to a halt by the barn, in his mind he had already sold all of their liquid assets, booked a train west and started a new life.

Sarah came to the barn as he was unhitching the horse. She was such a soothing sight to Ira's heavy heart. He pulled her close. They walked hand in hand to the house. Ira sat her down on the porch.

"We have a lot to talk about," he said.

Sarah swallowed hard not sure what he was going to tell her. She listened intently. Her blood too, ran chill when he talked about the gambler. Even more so when he talked about the sorrel gelding. Sarah knew first-hand what a wretch that gambler was. She was so glad when she and her siblings were not at her uncle's any longer. But he knew where she was.

Then at the end of the conversation, Ira with tears in his eyes added, "and I didn't get you that blue dress at the dry goods store. I sure wanted to," he said. Sarah's heart melted. Oh how she loved this gentle, kind hearted man.

"Okay" she said. "We will start preparing to leave tomorrow."

Ira sold his house to Alonzo for a small sum and Ozro gave him some cash for his part of the ranch. It wasn't a lot but what they gave him would get them west and give them a new start. Ira also had the money from the 7 geldings that he sold when this whole "leaving town incident" started. They said tear filled good byes to a beloved family.

They arrived in Denver with the light wagon, the stud that Tom Ketchum had traded for which he now called Black Jack, and 10 darling mares. Ira left Sarah and the kids in the wagon and he went to check the horses onto a cattle car and booked their passage to Rattlesnake Junction, which had recently changed to Mountain Home, Idaho Territory.

Sarah's siblings bailed out of the wagon and headed up the boardwalk to see the sights of this big city. She treated the kids to an ice cream at the parlor. Her brother was caring for Inez. Just around the corner was that dry goods store and that blue dress that Ira kept talking about. She wanted to go sneak a peek.

When she got to the store window she could see it. Ira was right it was beautiful. It was a color like a robin's egg only darker. She began to imagine how she might look in it and she could faintly see her reflection in the big window. She began primping and holding her hair up and imagining herself in the dress. She didn't see that drunk man staggering down the street. The drunk stopped to watch Sarah. "How ironic does my life get," he laughed to himself. He walked up behind Sarah and forced her body hard against the store window.

"You remember me honey?" he smothered her with his hot, putrid smelling breath.

It was her uncle's friend, the gambler who Ira's horse had beaten. She tried to turn her face to look at him and tried to struggle from his arms. She wouldn't scream. She was glad the kids were in the ice cream parlor. Last thing she wanted to do was to cause scene. They might hear her and come wandering out. Her brothers might try to do something to protect her and that might not turn out well. She tried to start a conversation with the drunk hoping that then he might loosen his grip. But all he could say was that he warned her half pint husband what he would do if he caught him in his territory again.

"Guess he didn't git the message I left for him at the livery," he said.

"Oh he got it alright, takes a big man to slit a horses throat, don't it?" she muttered coolly.

She felt like she was about to pass out from his stench and standing so uncomfortably against the wall. Just as she was thinking she couldn't take this any longer, she felt and heard a loud thud. The gambler fell to the ground and she quickly stepped away from his grasp. Sarah then saw her rescuer. Ira returning from the station had walked up behind them. He had pulled his pistol and hit the gambler in the back of the head.

"I guess Sam Colt really did make the great equalizer," he smiled. "I am sure glad I didn't have to shoot that snake though."

Ira and Sarah quickly gathered their family. He took them into the station to purchase the tickets. The train would depart in a couple of hours. He left his family and their trunks in the station and left to deliver the horse and the wagon to the livery. He had sold the whole outfit for a good price. The livery man had been good to him over the years.

Ira was busy unharnessing the horse when a couple of men came by. Clouds were forming in the sky and Ira had been hurrying to beat the coming storm. He looked up as a man with a growling voice: none other than his gambler "friend" began to poke fun at him.

"Told you not to be in my territory Shorty," he smirked, "and you've gone and disobeyed me again."

With that comment his companions began to laugh. Ira took a deep breath. He was scared. He had left his pistol in the wagon box several feet away. He wasn't that great of a shot anyway, but it might help him. "Why won't this guy leave me alone?" he shouted in his mind.

By this time the gambler and his friend had come over to the side of the horse where Ira was unhitching the singletree. He was definitely out to settle a score. The hair on the back of Ira's neck stood straight up. He knew these dogs were out for his blood. The gambler lunged for him, but swift on his feet, Ira leaped out of his way. The gambler's friend however was behind Ira and he shoved him hard back toward the gambler. There was no way Ira could reach the wagon box to get his pistol so he began to search the area for some other weapon to defend himself. The gambler's next lunge knocked Ira into the horse. The frightened little gelding skittishly pulled out of the way leaving the unattached harness and singletree on the ground at Ira's feet. He quickly grabbed the singletree and lifted it high in the air. The gambler's friend moved out of the way. The singletree crashed hard against the gambler's head. He fell forward on to his stomach. As he lay face down on the ground, Ira took full advantage of the gambler's inability to fight. He landed another forceful blow to the upper back. By standers heard Ira mutter as the blows came down.

"Don't ever call me Shorty again!"

"Don't ever slit one of my horses throats again!"

Then with a crushing two handed blow to the lower legs Ira breathed forcefully, "and don't you ever," he landed another blow, "ever touch my wife again!"

By this time the men in the crowd pulled Ira away from the gambler. In all reality though, Ira was done. He had beaten that dog for all the reasons he had built up inside. The crowd agreed that the gambler had provoked this whole thing and they let Ira peacefully finish his business. He leaned on the wagon box and took a deep breath trying to calm his shaking hands. Then he stood up straight and tall, went into the livery to deliver the horse and the wagon as promised.

Finally, he stopped outside the train station and tried to compose himself again. He didn't want Sarah to know what had just happened but at the same time he really needed to let Levi know. He checked to see if he looked like he had been in a fight, then he went into the station to meet his family.

Chapter 6
Idaho Territory 1886

Two days after leaving Denver, the train with her weary passengers pulled into Mountain Home. The map of the Idaho Territory that Ira had gotten at the land patent office still had this place identified as Rattlesnake Station. Sarah had not been impressed when Ira told her that he had booked tickets to get off at Rattlesnake. Before leaving the station Ira went to the Western Union Office. He was worried about the way they left Denver and really felt he needed to warn Levi. He sketched out a bare bones message that read;

Gambler tried me again. Watch yerself. Reached the Idaho, Ira.

Even though the telegraph was expensive Ira had to get him a warning. He also penned a longer letter which described more in detail the events that transpired. That letter he sent by mail from the station.

Black Jack and the mares were unloaded at the stockyards on the outskirts of town. Ira and his family walked the short distance to gather them. Ira had packed his saddle and two others and a couple of extra bed rolls on the train with the horses. Sarah could ride now or any combination of the others. Ira had decided to quit calling the kids her siblings. Starting today a new start lay ahead of them. They were a family.

The man at the stockyards said that there was a wagon builder no more than a quarter mile from where Ira could get a much-needed wagon. The walking felt good especially after riding the train for so long. Sarah and the kids made a picnic in a shady spot near the wagon shop. Here she fed them the last of the food she had brought with them. They would get supplies after they got the wagon and harness. Ira told the wagon smith that he was looking for some good ranch land to homestead in the southern part of this territory. He asked the wagon man if he knew where the Sparks Harrell ranch might be. "In which state?" the man retorted. As Ira inquired further the man showed him a rough map but it was similar to the one he had purchased at the Denver office. Then the wagon builder told him that honestly he would have better luck hearing about the conquers and busts at the saloon down the street. Ira took a stroll.

Inside the saloon was dark and it took his eyes a moment to adjust. There were only a few customers but he saw one man sitting in the corner who honestly was the

oldest looking man that Ira had ever seen. Ira walked up close to the old man's stool.

"Ira Brackett is my name," he said as he held out his hand. "You look like a man who might know this country well. Could I buy you a whiskey for a little bit of your advice."

The man smiled at Ira. He only had one tooth in the front of his mouth. "Of course," he said. "Eatin is getting harder for me these days so beer is my main nutrient…Buy away."

Ira told him that he had come to this country looking for a good place to ranch and a new start for his family. The old man said that he had trapped beaver in every stream in this territory. When Ira asked specifically about good ranch land in the southern part of the territory the beaver trapper smiled.

He hobbled over to the doors and pointed to the south, "See them shiny mountains?"

Ira looked to the south and did see a range of mountains.

"There," the trapper said, "is where God runs his cows, I hear."

Back inside he drew for Ira a rough map of what he called the Three Creeks country. Ira bought the trapper a couple more drinks and thanked him for his thoughts. He took the map and left the saloon.

He found his family at the feed supply store. Sarah had bought flour and beans and bacon. She found a really good deal on a cast iron cooker that a family leaving for Oregon had left. They bought five hens and a rooster and an old jersey milk cow. As for the chickens, she used Ira's knife to clip one wing so that they couldn't fly. Outside of town they made camp for the night. Sarah enjoyed having her new cooking set up and food to cook with. She might have enjoyed the whole experience more but was in a few short months expecting their third child.

The next day they pulled camp at first daylight. They were all eager to see the new country here. Still heading south they camped that night near Bruneau. A couple more days travel, always south looking for the big shining mountains. One day Sarah remarked that the mountain ahead of them looked like a big eye shining, watching over this country.

"Must be God's eye," she said.

That made Ira smile. They hadn't seen other homesteaders for most of the way. Sarah thought that the kids might like to have neighbors around. Honestly she might like that too. On the train there was much talk about the Bannocks being on the raid and their family had seen what the Indian raids were like from living in Colorado. They spent the night near a meadow on Big Flat Creek. At least that's what they figured it was called from the beaver trappers map. Here someone had built a big log home with barns and horse corrals. A short distance to the south they came to a small stream that they thought to call their own. A very tired, very pregnant Sarah said she had gone far enough.

Ira set promptly to work building a small shanty to keep their family safe from the winter cold. Come springtime however, they would find that they had too many neighbors and that all the good ground had been staked. In this Idaho Territory they would stake out several places before they found the right place to call home.

Shiny Mountains

Three Creeks Area

Stage Stop

spring

Smith Crossing

↑ South

Clover Crossing

River

Winter Loop

Bruneau 11

△ mountain Home

End of Chap. 6.

Chapter 7
Bige looking for a new home
1898

Life on the Duncan family ranch in Knickerbocker sure wasn't the same these days. The place that old man Duncan had homesteaded in Texas had originally been more than enough to make a good living for his growing family. But as Abijah Sr. and his wife Martha's family of 7 surviving children grew there were lots of mouths to feed. When the oldest of their sons, Abijah Jr. (Bige) married Nancy Blake Ketchum back in '79 there still seemed like lots of opportunity. Bige was planning to work hard alongside his brothers Jim, Tap and Richard. They would buy several of the neighbor's places as they came up for sale and with their hard work they would make them all as productive as this central Texas ground could be. That seemed to be working great until Jim, Tap and Richard all wandered off to New Mexico on a cattle drive. Tap took a long time recovering from a beating he took in a bar there. That changed him, inside and he just wasn't quite the same. Richard got hung for a crime he didn't do. He was just trying to make a living and a future for his family. That hanging seemed to take the heart and the will out of the old man. Now that Jim and Tap had both left for the Idaho Territory, Bige was thinking more and more that perhaps he should sell out and head north to those Idaho grasslands too.

Nancy had given birth 9 times and 7 of those kids were still alive. Two of them had died at just two years old. Bige had a lot of mouths to feed. Last year he had gotten a letter from his brother Jim telling him about the great life he and the new wife had found. Tap also was doing well. He was working hard and was a cow boss for a large ranch in Nevada. Eager to see if this new found territory where Jim and Tap seemed to be thriving could be the makings of a new home for him, Bige kissed his wife Nancy and bought a train ticket to Wells, Nevada.

He sent a letter to his brothers and Tap met him at the station. The reunion was sweet. They talked for several hours. Catching up on life. Tap drew Bige several maps of good cow country that he had traveled while he was with Sparks-Harrell. Tap said that he was looking to sell his own ranch and cattle. He and Ollie and the kids were headed south.

"Why's that?" Bige asked.

Tap said that Idaho was too cold for Ollie and too hot for him. Back in1894 he said he got in a bar fight in Bruneau. He had to shoot a man to stay alive.

"You know, Bige, when they beat me near to death in New Mexico," he breathed out slowly, I vowed I would never let anything like that happen to me again."

He looked at Bige hoping for some absolution and Bige quickly gave it to him. "A man's gotta do what he's gotta do. What happened?" he then asked.

"I got lucky at cards," Tap smiled. "Been to Mountain Home to sell some steers. They sold well and on my way home I stopped off at Bruneau to quench my thirst. In the saloon there was a friendly game of cards in the makes and I was asked to join in. Lady luck just kept dealing me the best cards." He was smiling at that memory as if it were the best thing he could remember.

"I won and I won until that gambler who owned the game lost it all to me. He was pretty miffed as he left. I think he figured me for an easy take. " He stopped and thought about what he wanted to say next. "Anyways, I began to think I needed to head on out to make my camp for the night. "

Looking squarely at his brother, he continued, "I paid for my drinks and walked slowly to outside. As my shadow reached the doors, somebody opened up shooting. A bullet hit my belt buckle and saved my life. I dove to the floor and rolled close to the open doors. I was pulling my pistols out as I rolled. I looked up in the doorway and there stood the gambler whose money I had just won. I shot him before he could get off another shot."

"It was self-defense and they let me go, but I didn't really care to travel that country much after that." Bige nodded thoughtfully.

He asked his brother to come with him to look for some prospective places he could buy if he sold the home place in Knickerbocker. Tap liked the sound of that especially since he too was in a quest for new ranch country to call his own.

They took the train west to Elko and began to inquire about ranches for sale. They found a few but kept hearing a common thread about a new bank in Nevada. Seems that this new bank held most of the business and many mortgages for the ranches in the northern part of the state. The brothers decided to ride the train further west to the town where this bank was. A cow town on the railroad called Winnemucca.

They got off the train and headed up the street to the First National Bank. Inside, the bank they said they were looking to purchase a ranch. Shortly, they were conversing with a pleasant man named George Nixon. Nixon said he was a rancher himself and his place was just shortly out of town. The Duncans spent the next several days accompanying that bank president to various ranches. Some that he held mortgages on and some he loaned operating capital, some that he just knew were for sale.

One ranch in particular that he showed them piqued Bige's interest. It was owned by a wealthy widow who had been losing money for years. As he and Tap retired to the boarding house after their tour with Mr. Nixon, Bige spent all evening and several of the wee morning hours penciling out a rough plan that might make that ranch work. He had run it over and over in his mind: he knew what he could do to make it work. He could sell the home place in San Saba for the down payment but he would have to borrow a substantial amount of money for operating capital.

Bige slept very little for the rest of the night. In the morning, he and Tap went to the bank to talk the plan over with Nixon. Nixon said that he felt he was a good judge of character. He often made loans based more on character than even collateral. He told the brothers that they looked like men of their word who would do what they said they would do.

Bige was nervous but encouraged by Nixon's words as he presented his plan to his newfound friend. When he came to the part about the money he would need to borrow, Nixon politely laughed.

"The only way you could get that kind of money out of this bank," he paused, "would be to rob it." He snorted.

A sort of stillness hung in the air. Tap wondered if he knew just who he was talking to.

Now it was Bige and Tap's turn to laugh. They looked at each other.

"That could perhaps be arranged," they both said at the same time. Tap raised his eyebrows at the curiosity of this conversation. As they finished the last of their discussions, Bige left his address with Nixon just in case he changed his mind on the loan. They shook hands and agreed to stay in touch.

As they left, Nixon looked studiously at the addresses and the names....San Saba Texas....Abijah Duncan didn't ring familiar but...Tap Duncan. George kept running the names over and over in his mind. He had come to Winnemucca as an official with the railroad. He remembered hearing about a man named Tap Duncan that at times was reported to ride with the Wild Bunch Gang. He was reported to have been involved in various bank and train robberies throughout New Mexico and the west. Nixon smiled at the irony of this day.

Bige and Tap rode the train back to Wells. There Tap got off and headed north back to Three Creek. Not having found the new start for his family that he had hoped for, Bige headed back to Texas.

A few short months later, Bige received a letter from Winnemucca, Nevada. It simply read: "Wish to talk over business deal. Know more about your family now. George Nixon. Meet in Denver."

Bige was more than a little nervous. After he had returned from his trip, he had given up the thought of selling San Saba and he was nestling in here looking for new workable opportunities. Now this could be a shot.

Arrangements were made and a short time later they did meet at the train station in Denver.

They went to dinner and finally Nixon began opening up to Bige what he thought was the ranch deal. Nixon began, "You know, I told you before that in my bank we make more loans based on character than even collateral."

Bige was getting very excited at this point. "Does that mean you changed your mind and you are gonna loan me all that money?" Bige asked and he felt his legs shaking under the table. Nixon got real quiet.

"No." He said. "Because you seem to me to be a man who can and will do what he says he will do," Nixon paused, "I am gonna offer you the deal of a lifetime." He leaned his head over the table closer to Bige. In a quiet whisper he said, "My bank is in trouble." There was a long pause. Whether Nixon was trying to compose his thoughts or his emotions, Bige wasn't sure. Nixon rubbed his chin hard with the palm of his hands, swallowed hard then continued now in a more authoritative voice.

"The only way I can come out of this is if my bank is robbed."

"You can have all the money. But I have hard and fast rules. I don't want anyone hurt. No one can ever know I was involved. It would ruin me personally and politically. I want you to get a few good men to help you. They have to be disciplined, not get drunk and throw their money around or brag about their deed. We have to do this right so that no one will ever know what happened." Then he added," I have heard that some of your family are braggarts and can't be trusted, Don't use them." He went on, "If you don't get caught with indisputable evidence, I promise to never identify you. Also, I can and will steer the authorities away from you."

Bige sat for a long time and just looked at Nixon without saying anything. Finally he took his hat off and scratched his head. "Well this is a shock." he said. "I can tell you honestly that I have never done anything like this before, even though I know some who have. I will need to think it over."

Nixon swallowed hard and said, "I was hoping you would say that. I need only cautious men to do this deed. Do it right so we will all stay out of trouble." The next morning after a sleepless night, Bige met Nixon for breakfast. He told him that he needed some time to visit with his brother Tap, and he would get back to him soon.

Chapter 8
Visit with Tap

The last letter that the family had received from Tap said that he and Ollie and the kids were in the Mohave country near Hackberry in Arizona. Bige sent word that he needed to talk to him about the business deal at the bank. Tap was really curious and eager to see his brother. Bige hadn't realized how much he missed having his brothers around. With Jim in Idaho, Tap in Arizona, and Dick in the graveyard at San Saba, he was the only son left to care for his parents and the family ranch. Bige was pleased to see how well Tap was doing and that his ranch here was substantial. Ollie fed the brothers a good meal and they went out on the porch to talk.

"What's this about the bank deal?" Tap asked curiously.

Bige took a deep breath and began, "You remember when we were in Winnemucca, Tap? When I asked Nixon for a loan, he smiled and he commented that the only way to get that kind of money out of his bank, would be to rob it." Tap leaned back and laughed, "Yeah that was pretty funny."

Bige looked very seriously at Tap. Then he almost whispered, "He asked us to rob it."

Tap had just taken a drink and spattered out the whiskey in his mouth. "What did you say Bige?" He asked.

This time Bige said it forcefully, "Nixon asked us to rob the bank."

"His bank?" Tap asked incredulously.

"Yeah his bank," Bige replied. Tap leaned forward.

"A set up you think?"

"No," Bige replied. "He said he was in real trouble and he is in a tough spot, with his political aspirations and all, a failure at his bank would kill him. A robbery is the only way he can save face."

Tap leaned back on his chair. He could see by the look on his brother's face that this was not a joke. Tap looked up at the nighttime sky. He held his hands out, "God is smiling down on me." He laughed. Then he asked Bige "What did you tell him?"

Bige said simply, "I told him I would have to talk to you." Tap and Bige sat in silence for a long time.

Tap thought back through several incidents in his life. Times when life it seems hadn't dealt him a fair hand. The trail drive when he was just 16.

Times were tough and money was hard to come by. The Duncan boys were all excellent horsemen. They would catch wild horses make trades for other and ride anything with four legs and hair. It was one thing they could do and do well. But in their part of Texas there wasn't much for young men to do so when a trail herd started up to take cattle north to New Mexico, the Duncans were among the first to sign up. The trail driving was hot, dirty work. Water even to drink was scarce. Other herds that had passed this way had grazed nearly all the grass. After 3 long dusty weeks on the trail with no place to wash, sleeping on the ground and eating food that camp cooky bragged would make you sick, they finally reached the trail head. They had earned every cent of the money that the paymaster issued them.

What an adventure for a boy thinking he was turning into a man. In high spirits Tap's brothers took him to the saloon for his first taste of real whiskey even before they found a bath, some clean clothes and a soft bed for the night in this cow town.

Dick, Jim and Bige taking him to the saloon for a drink of whiskey should have been a simple rite of passage. But some onery New Mexican raunchies began making fun of them for dressing and smelling like Texans. One big man in particular who didn't smell so good himself took particular offense to the Duncans. Full of fire water and mean as a badger this man singled Tap out.

While Tap himself was a good sized young man and thickly muscled, he was about 4 inches shorter and probably 50 pounds lighter than the New Mexican. When he accusingly called Tap a momma's boy, Tap thought that was about the stupidest thing he had ever heard. And being young and untempered, he dared to say as much out loud. The bully with the whiskey in his gut took that as a challenge. He knocked Tap off his bar stool before he could even say sorry, although he hadn't planned to anyway.

Already light headed from his first few drinks of whiskey, Tap tried to scramble to his feet but stumbled in the attempt. When the Duncan brothers moved off their stool to help their little brother the drunk man's friends drew pistols warning them to stay back. The man who had knocked Tap down kicked him first in the stomach with the sharp point of his boot. That stung like nothing he had ever felt before. He kept wondering why this was happening to him. Next, he kicked Tap in the chin and the throat. Blood was gushing and Tap was panicking. He couldn't breathe. The next kick was more of a stomp to his face and at that point the brothers had seen enough. Dick quickly grabbed one gunman's arm and slammed it hard on the bar. The other brothers took that as their cue and disarmed the other gunmen. Dick forcefully knocked the man down who was beating up Tap. He stepped hard on his throat and said he would kill him if he ever messed with any of his family ever again. He took the end of his pistol and hit the drunk hard across the face. Dick was sure it broke that man's nose. Tap had become unconscious at some point but woke later laying out in the street hurting like he had never hurt. His head was in Dick's lap and he was dipping his scarf in the water trough wiping Tap's swollen bloody face. Bige stood nearby with his gun out promising to shoot anyone who came their way. It was weeks before Tap recovered. Lucky for the Duncan brothers, there was a family in town that offered to let them stay in their barn for as long as Tap needed. Jim sold their packhorse for money to otherwise nurse him back to the living.

Tap did have his rite of passage to manhood however before they left New Mexico. With some of the money he earned on the trail drive, he acquired a colt pistol that seldom, if ever wasn't carried at his side.

He thought about being in Texas, ranching with his dad and brothers. It was a good time in life. He remembered how his brother Dick had been working hard and was moving his life forward. He had driven cattle trails, worked for neighbors and saved. He finally had enough money saved to buy the Williamson's place not far from their family home. Here he was about to start a ranch of his own. There was a cute neighbor girl who had stolen his heart. There was just one last task before he would start his new life. As a part of the Williamson's sale Dick had agreed to help them move to their new home in Mexico. Walter Landers had agreed to ride along with him to make sure the Williamson's got to Mexico safely. Near Eagle Pass, Dick agreed to ride on ahead and scout out the best trail. After two weeks in Mexico, finding the best route, Dick returned to find a message from the family that they had changed their minds and were headed to California. It turned out that someone had murdered the family and taken their wagon. As Dick returned home he was surprised to find that his dad, Abijah sr. and Tap had met a man with a Mitchell wagon that he wanted to sell for a good price. They knew the value of this kind of wagon and eagerly bought it. The seller claimed that his wife had run off with a gambler and he wanted to sell the wagon so he could travel light to California. The Williamson's had a wagon just like that one. Rangers were looking for it and when they arrested Dick he tried to tell them what had happened. But they were sure they had found the man who committed the crime and they were gonna see him hanged. The only question was were they gonna hang Abijah Sr., Tap and Dick or just Dick? Tap knew but for the grace of God he would have joined his brother at the hanging tree. Dick did protest that they were hanging an innocent man. They told him to shut it or there would be a hangin for three. Dick calmly and quietly went to his rope. That miscarriage of justice would haunt and shape the Duncan family, especially Tap. Duncan family blood runs deep.

He thought how he had been accused of things he never did. True, he killed that man in Bruneau in self-defense. But it was self-defense and after his beating in New Mexico and Dick's hanging, when he bought that colt pistol he vowed to use it to care for himself and his own. He didn't go looking for trouble but if you crossed him....you were messing with a rattlesnake.

The ranch here in Arizona was good. Ollie and the kids were happy and yeah he was too. He would like his ranch to grow faster, but it was good. He had been to Winnemuccca and he had seen the fliers that advertised the money that the bank held.

"That much money could start up a couple of good size ranches." he said mostly in answer to his own thoughts.

Bige smiled. "Indeed it would!"

"Maybe this will change our family luck." Tap was getting more excited. "Let me show you Bige how we can do this."

"We need more than just us, three men for the inside, one to get the money and two others to flank him, and we need a horse handler for the getaway."

As soon as Tap said horse handler his thoughts immediately turned to Ira. Tap made the remark that in a life

or death situation, there wasn't a man alive he'd rather depend on to get him a secure mount than Ira Brackett.

"Ira's a real straight arrow though," He was thinking aloud again.

"Okay, who else, then?" Bige asked eager to know his brother's thoughts.

"Well now just wait a minute," Tap rubbed his chin. "There might be an angle that we can use to get him." Tap's mind began to wander. Then he said, "I will go to Idaho and talk to him." Bige curiously consented.

Then Tap continued, "I will enlist Jim while I am there. Since he married that sweet Lizzy Helsley he has settled some but he's our blood, he will help us out."

"So we maybe have four?" Bige asked. "We'll need another."

They both thought on Bige's brothers'-in-law. But Sam Ketchum was in jail about to be hung and Tom, well he was having some troubles of his own. Also with Nixon's strict rules about men that wouldn't get drunk and throw money around and about keeping mouths shut... the Ketchums weren't even candidates. Some might have said they enjoyed bragging about their robberies nearly as much as they enjoyed the money from them.

A big smile grew across Bige's face, he said, "However, my other in law, Green Berry Ketchum...now he could keep his mouth shut. I think that quietly he has shared in a lot of the fortune from the Ketchum gang's thievery. He has quietly buried it away in his ranch and never peeped a word. Won't either even on his dying day, I think."

"Ok we sort of have it settled, you go, Bige to recruit Green Berry and I will head back to Idaho and get Jim and Ira on board."

Chapter 9
Tap Goes to Idaho

Tap bought a ticket and hopped the train to Wells, Nevada. He bought a horse and some supplies at the livery and headed north to O'Neil Basin. As he rode through the sage brush, his mind began rolling out all the memories that his place held for him.

He had been lucky landing the cow boss job for the Sparks-Harrell. He was surprised one day as he was returning from cow camp and he stopped at Old Man Faraday's store to have a drink. Who should be at the store other than his old friend from Colorado, Ira Brackett. The two men chatted for most of the afternoon. Ira told Tap that he had been going down to the Inside Desert, just east of the canyon to gather wild horses and it had been quite profitable. That horse herd on the desert had been better than harvesting apples. He could get a few new colts every years and come back and a new crop had grown. In a few more days he was headed out and wondered if Tap might like to join him. True to his roots, Ira was making a living taming and breaking wild horses. Tap said that he had been to cow camp for several weeks and needed a few days with his family but then he would be game for a roundup. That started a profitable venture for both men.

On one of Ira's horse runs to the desert the men found themselves on the 71 Desert scouting for signs of the horse herd. When they camped that night, Tap brought out his flask of whiskey to share with Ira. The campfire felt good against the night's late springtime air. They hadn't even cut a sign on the horse trail that day and Ira wondered if they ought to head to Bruneau the next day to see if the herd was closer to the Snake River.

Tap hesitated. "Uhhhh, not sure I wanna go there, Ira" he said. "I got in a mess of trouble there a while ago." Ira searched Tap's face for a further explanation. "A gambler got his feathers ruffled when I beat his game. He tried me and I had to shoot him before he shot me. It was self-defense but he's got kin who don't see it that way. Why some men aren't better than rabid dogs I will never understand but why in the hell is it always me who has to tangle with 'em?"

Ira's blood ran cold in his veins. He had tried as of late not to think about that dog of a gambler in Denver. Made life so tough for him, he just got his family outta town. Just two years after he left for the Idaho, he got the sickening news: Levi had been murdered in the streets of Arvada, Colorado near Denver. Looking back he wished he would have finished beating the life out of that gambler when he had the chance. Levi would probably be alive yet today. Tears stung his eyes every time he thought on it and here it was 10 years later.

Tap took a long sip of whiskey. "Never told anyone this Ira, but after those rangers hung my brother Dick at Eagles pass, I..I couldn't sleep." He was silent for a long time. Finally he continued, "seems that every time I shut my eyes all I could see was Dick heading for those gallows and telling those rangers they were hangin' an innocent man." Tap stopped and took another long sip. He put his hand on the pistol at his side touching it like a trusted friend. He continued, "I found 'em and I just took care of 'em." His voice trailed off. Ira looked at him wondering if that meant what he thought it meant. Tap then cleared his throat and stood up, looking at the stars that lit up the sky and he shouted, "and I have felt better every day since...I love ya, Dick!" He guzzled down the last of the whiskey and threw the flask into the dark as if he was trying to make it all disappear into the black chilly night. There was no doubt what Tap had meant. He had found those rangers who pinned that murder on Dick and he evened the score.

Ira wondered how he might feel if his brother's killers were dealt with. After a long time wrapped up in his own thoughts, Ira said," Well if I had the means, I'd send someone to clean up those filthy dogs in Denver." He then sighed, "But now I have mouths to feed my own as well as Levi's kids." Then he added, "No time for what ifs." Ira crawled into his bedroll. Ira and Tap returned from running horses this time, busted. The herd they thought must have gone on north to the Snake.

THIS conversation was being run over and over in Tap's mind as his horse traveled the miles to Three Creek.

He smiled to himself. He did know of an angle to get Ira to handle the horses for the robbery. That is, if anything would.

Out of O'Neil Basin, Tap followed Canyon Creek to the source at the top of the mountain. Many a time he had brought cattle on this trail as they came to the trailhead at Deeth. He was making in his mind the map that would get them home from Winnemucca with the gold. When he dropped over the mountain and down to Three Creek he had played over and over in his mind the plan.

The plan for the route.

The plan for the getaway.

But most important, and at hand was the plan to get Jim and Ira on board. He hoped it would all fall in to place.

Tap's first stop was at Jim's ranch just down the creek from Faraday's store. Tap had sent a letter to Jim telling him he was coming but he hadn't received it. So he was greatly surprised to see his dear brother riding down his lane.

Emotions burned hot inside Tap as he looked around at what had been, just a few years ago, his home. He and Jim shared more than blood. They shared life experiences...good and not so good. He truly missed his brother, the bond and the life that they had shared. He really did love this cow country. Anger stirred inside him as he thought about letting some mad dogs chase him out of this place. Arizona was good to him and his family but he did miss it here.

Tap asked Jim to saddle up and ride to Faraday's with him for a drink. There they got a drink and wandered out to sit in the sun but also to have a private place to talk.

"So Tap, What's up?" Jim asked curiously.

Tap smiled. "Do I need a reason to come to see my favorite brother?" He asked.

Jim smiled and said, "You and yours are a good 1000 miles from here and I look out my window one day and you are riding up to my door. What's up?"

Tap began. "I have a business proposition for you." Then he continued. "You remember a while back when Bige was thinking of selling San Saba, and we went to check out some ranches in Nevada?" Jim was getting curious. Tap continued, "We met a banker in Winnemucca, he owns the First National. He's a young aspiring politician. Seems he has kept in contact with Bige. They met in Denver a while ago. " Tap stopped, took a drink and continued. "Nixon, that banker, told Bige that his bank was in trouble." Tap studied Jim's face, "He asked us to rob it."

Jim hooted. "The bank? He wants US to rob HIS bank?"

Tap nodded he was grinning from ear to ear. "Well, why us?" Jim wondered out loud.

Tap looked at him and both men laughed at the question that he had just posed. "So are you gonna do it?" He asked. It seemed like curiosity and excitement were starting to creep into Jim's voice.

Tap studied Jim's face trying to decide what to say next, finally he just said, "We can't do it without you Jim."

Jim thought about how ranching was getting tougher and tougher on him. He was beginning to feel all the miles he had spent in the saddle, all the bar room brawls, and hard knocks that life had handed him. He thought about the pleasant things that life with Lizzy had brought him even in this short time. He thought about how she wanted to buy the

Faraday's store and run it for their family business. If only they would make enough money. Jim smiled at the thought. 'How much would this robbery be worth exactly?" He asked. Jim was in, with both feet too, it seemed.

Tap was pleased that the meeting with Jim went so well. His next task would perhaps require more finesse.

He arrived at Ira's place later that afternoon. He, too was glad see his old friend. He invited him to dinner which Tap obliged. After they ate however, Tap insisted that they go outside to talk. He hated to leave Sarah out of the conversation but she couldn't, wouldn't have any part of this. So Ira said that he wanted to show Tap the most recent horses he had gathered. Out at the barn Ira looked at Tap. "You got troubles?" he asked.

"No," Tap replied. "I do have a proposition though." Ira looked curiously at Tap.

"Yeah?" he asked.   Even though he had rehearsed this speech over and over in his mind nearly every mile as he rode up this way he still wasn't sure how he was gonna spit it out.

"Ira," he began, "You remember when we were running horses a while back and you wanted to go to Bruneau, and I told you that I couldn't go there?" Ira was really starting to worry about what kind of trouble his friend was in now.

Tap continued, "You remember the conversation we had about, you know about Dick and those rangers?"

Ira remembered that well.   He could still see a satisfied and vindicated Tap standing there in the dark telling him that he had evened the score for his brother.

"Yeah, I remember it, Tap."

Tap took a deep breath and said, "I am here Ira to offer you a deal, my friend." He said.

He looked very serious and said, "Ira please hear me out before you say anything, will you promise me?"

Ira pulled off his hat and rubbed his nearly bald head. He didn't want to promise something he couldn't keep. "Okay, I will listen."

Tap told Ira about the trip that he and Bige had taken to Winnemucca looking at ranches. He talked about George Nixon and Ira, true to his word, didn't say a thing. Finally when he came to the part about Nixon asking Bige to rob the bank, Ira did smile.

"Why are you telling me this Tap?" he asked.

Tap folded his hands and simply said. "To do this we need someone to handle the getaway horses."

Ira raised his eyebrows and settled back against the barn wall. He shook his head.

"I ain't never done anything like that and I am sure too damn old to start!" He chuckled at the thought. "I could always use more money, but in all reality I have all I need."

Tap smiled solemnly. "You know Ira..." Tap cleared his throat, "this conversation we are having right here and now, it ain't about the money."

He kicked thoughtfully at the dirt with the toe of his boot. "I am offering you a way to feel better every day....just like I did about Dick."

Ira looked at him very seriously. He thought on what had just been said then asked, "What exactly are you sayin', Tap?"

Tap looked at Ira very seriously and then said, "I am saying what you think I am saying Ira. Quite simply, you help me solve my problem and I will see that yours is taken care of. "

Ira didn't say anything for a while. Then he moved forward and said, "Denver, you mean?"

Tap nodded, "Yes, I mean Denver."

Chapter 10
Every Man Has a Job

Late afternoon and everyone gathered at the camp down by the river. They were going to go over the plan just one more time. Tap took charge of the group. He said that while it was Bige's meeting with Nixon that had set this whole game in motion, and while every man there was capable, he felt that he had more knowledge of this sort of thing than any of the others. This group needed a man in charge and if someone else really wanted the job, Tap said, they could have it. All agreed that Tap was to be the man.

They would enter the bank at noon, go in heavily armed. Every man then checked his several pistols. There would not be time to reload, if things went bad.

.After checking and loading their guns, they placed them on the ground in front of them. Tap started around the circle.

"Ok, Bige," he said. "What's your job?"

Bige said he was to be out in front of the First National, tell the others when it was time to enter the bank and try to keep anyone from walking in on the robbery. After the robbery he would help Nixon do crowd control and direct the posse. Other than that he would just sit around until it was all over. He smiled.

Tap looked at him sternly, "Wrong, Bige." He said. "Yes, you'll be out in front and tell us when to go in, but you will do whatever it takes to keep anyone from coming in! I do mean whatever. Block the door, start a fight, whatever it takes."

Tap looked at everybody, "If someone comes in, it is more than likely that someone will get hurt." Now he looked at Bige, "You will be by yourself," Tap swallowed hard then continued, "The rest of us have back up, but you are on your own." Tomorrow you will take that fancy blooded sorrel gelding. Ira said he is a true powerhouse. You'll leave him just down the street at the ready if you need him. Your job is probably the most dangerous and I want you to be able to get out if you must. Remember to saddle him with that plain saddle Ira picked up on the way down here. Now as we leave town, what do you do?" Tap asked Bige.

"I will echo Nixon's efforts to direct the posse. I will try to help him get the volunteers to the train."

"That is right." Tap said. Then he added, "Nixon will work to get them to take the train thinking that they can cut us off at Golconda." Tap smiled, "And that should give us the head start that we need to disappear."

"Ok," Tap continued, "When we get inside let me do the talking."

He looked at Jim and Green Berry, "You all will cover my back. I will have the money bags and tell Nixon and the tellers what to do. The vault should be open and I will clean it out then the teller's drawers. If there is too much to carry, Jim, you will help me. After the money is bagged we will take everyone out the back door and hold them until we are mounted and ready to roll out. "

"Sounds good, Tap," Jim said. "I will cover your back just like I always have. I will follow your lead, just tell me what to do and I will make sure it happens."

Green Berry was holding on to his shotgun and Tap smiled at the look of him. "Green," he said, "You will be my enforcer."

"You'll have your scatter gun and you will look scary. Make it crystal clear to everyone that if they want to be a hero...they will be a dead hero."

"You can't leave any room for chance, if someone thinks that there might be a chance we will get someone hurt... us included. No one wants that. Are we clear?"

Tap got a bit softer in his tone and then continued, "You are all my family and I promise that each and every one of you is going home to your wife and family."

Green Berry looked at Tap and grinned. "You are only asking me to act natural, after dealing with Tom and Sam, I can put fear in most anyone." He laughed.

"Ira," Tap breathed deeply. "Your job started weeks ago. Compliments to you, my friend." Tap smiled. "I don't know how you picked these horses, no two look alike. You tell me they can run and I trust you completely. My dad told me years ago that some people just know horse flesh. The story goes that an average settler can ride a horse hard and fast, 25 miles before he drops dead. The cavalry, with their travel routine can go 40 miles with the same horse. A good horseman, which we all are, can take that same horse 75. A Comanche buck with his knowledge of how to pace and motivate his horse can make 100 miles before that pony drops dead. Then he will jump off eat a chunk of raw horse flesh and run another 50. I personally don't want to run the last 50 miles." He smiled, "But with you pacing us Ira, we will be able to ride that 100 miles. Everyone in the camp was nodding and smiling.

Ira cleared his throat, "My job," he said as if to remind himself more than the rest, "I will be out back holding the horses. I will also make damn sure no one comes in that back door. There won't be any delay."

He looked at his friends, "As soon as you come out and get mounted up we will take off." You all will need to trust me and switch your horses or vary your pace as I tell you it's time."

Ira looked at the hobbled horses, "They may look like a motley bunch, but I promise you, they have the heart and will to travel. They will take us farther and faster than any set of horses around. You must take the horse I tell you to take, at the time I tell you to take it."

Ira shook his head and continued, "No questions, no back talk. If you do as I say, we will out run any posse, no one will be able to catch up with us or get ahead. I have cut the fence along the railroad in at least a dozen places, then we will be able to head north when we need to.

He smiled and said, "The last they will see of us will be our dust disappearing into the sage brush north and east of here."

Tap Duncan

Jim Duncan

Green Berry Ketchum Jr.

Ira Brackett

Abijay Duncan Jr.

Chapter 11
Leaving Winnemucca
Sept. 19, 1900

Out in the alley behind the First National, Ira waited with four of Nixon's finest blooded colts. Nixon's man had been training these colts for the California race tracks. They were fidgety. Ira didn't try to settle them. He was there to hold the horses and to make sure that no one walked into the bank on a robbery in session. Bige was settled on the window seat outside the front door. His job like Ira's was to prevent anyone from just wandering in from the front doors. Last night as they had gathered by their campfire going over their plans for at least the 47th time, Green Berry looked at them all and remarked that they should call themselves "The Over the Hill Gang." So Bige even carved himself a cane out of a willow stick from down by the creek. Ira smiled at that thought.

He quickly forced himself to focus back on the task at hand. Nervousness was twisting his stomach up. He circled the prancy little colts a couple of times to keep their blood up. He wanted them ready as soon as the boys came out to the alley. Everything depended on it. He hadn't waited long when the back door flew open and none other than George Nixon himself burst into the alley. Directly behind him was Tap with his .45 pistol pointed at Nixon's back. Next to him was a man who was obviously a teller. Jim was covering him with his own gun. Green Berry had the shotgun sighted on them. He had concealed it in his long coat when he entered the bank.

Tap gave Nixon a shove to the gravel. He left the gun cover to the others and grabbed from Ira his colt's reins and mounted quickly. At this point Green Berry pointed his gun at the prostrate men. "Guys", he said clearly, trying to cover his soft Texas drawl, "I'm just a bit nervous here, and I can promise you that if you move, it'll make my finger twitch and I am afraid this scatter gun'd blow a hole clean through ya, so you just lay there real quiet and still." Jim had mounted his horse and he and Tap were now covering the men while Green Berry got on. The speed with which they mounted was incredible. Those little colts were fresh and tired of standing around in the alley. As the robbers hit the steel to their sides they bounded off in a gallop.

Nixon watched them head out and disappear around the corner. At that point he jumped up and ran back inside the bank and grabbed his six shooter. Once again outside, he began firing in an effort to draw attention to the bank. He then ran towards the railhead and was calling for a posse.

He gathered several men and suggested that they all hop the train. The robbers, he pointed out were heading east. If he and his men would take the train they could beat the robbers up the Humboldt River and to next station. From there they could grab horses and ride back to catch those thieves. Bige who had been at the First National's front doors, joined the volunteers in following Nixon. His eagerness to follow the banker's lead helped influence the crowd.

Nixon and a few volunteers loaded up in the engineer's car. Excitedly they instructed him to head east as fast as this train could go. The train did at one point pass the bandits and soon after it did, they headed north, no longer following the tracks. As soon as they did, Nixon looked shocked. The volunteer's hope began to sink. They began to realize that the slight advantage the train could have given them was disappearing into the sagebrush sea. At the station in Golconda, Nixon and his horseless posse hopped a train headed back to Winnemucca. Bige, too, got off at this point as if to switch trains. But instead of hitting the cars headed back to Winnemucca, he slipped quietly through the crowd in the station and purchased a ticket to Elko. When Bige boarded for Elko, he smiled. The four riders by now would be changing their exhausted colts. With no one following them out of town, their lead was substantial and if they kept moving there would never be a trace.

Riding faster than any of them had ever done, Ira took the lead. True to the plan, they had headed east out of towns so as to draw the train. Then they headed north for several miles. About the time that the colts they were riding started to play out. They were only a short distance from the first of their exchange corrals, north and east of Golconda on Evans Creek. Those little colts had played well their part, they ran fast and hard.

At the corrals, acting on his experience from his pony express days, Ira told the men they had two minutes to change horse and hit the trail hard again. The four men had much incentive to make sure this getaway was successful. But even though they were hurrying they were steady in their preparations.

These new horses were fresh and green. Ira had chosen these carefully for their will and stamina. The men carefully tightened cinches after they set their saddles straight. A stop to retighten or reset would cost them precious getaway time. At this exchange they would leave those spent little colts and all would have two horses apiece; one to ride and a spare to travel. They also would take two packhorses they would load with their stashed gear. Back at the bank, more of the money was gold than they had realized. So here they roughly split the take just for hauling purposes. Tap ran his fingers through the gold in one of the bags just to hear the sweet sound of those gold pieces hitting together.

Tap was the first to get his new mount ready. He turned Nixon's colt loose in the sage and spent a few seconds searching the southwest horizon for signs of a posse. He didn't see one but he wasn't willing to gamble that it wasn't coming. As soon as the others got their mounts and turned the colts loose they hit the trail again fast and furiously. They headed north and east toward the town of Tuscarora. This leg of the journey would be fast but not as fast as the first.

They followed a wagon road east to Evans Creek and then later to Willow Creek. When later they would stop near Tuscarora, Winnemucca would be nearly 100 miles behind them. As the day wore on they began to feel more confident that Nixon had been true to his word and steered the posse from them.

The sun was sinking fast in the western sky. September nights in this high desert chilled off fast. The horsemen were now traveling more at a trot than a gallop allowing the horses to pick the best route. A stumble that might break a leg would be a cost they could not afford. About the time they figured they would have to stop for the night, much to their delight a full moon was rising in the southeastern sky. It was as bright as a reading light. Tap and Jim remembered a night many years ago when leaving New Mexico. They had that giant light in the sky to aid their flight. They shared a laugh as the riders traveled in.

Sometime later in the early morning, cold and beat, they stopped for just a few winks of sleep. There were a few scrub trees near the creek. Here they used their lariats to make a rope corral for the horses. While the bedrolls felt good against the September's night chill, not a man in the group slept well. As Ira closed his eyes, his mind kept playing over and over the events of the day. He had just participated in a bank robbery.

What would Sarah say if she found out? Well, he reasoned in his mind, we won't get caught and she nor would anyone else would ever find out. He would carry this secret to his grave, he vowed.

As the dawning sun began to color the sky, Ira pulled out of his bedroll. He was very eager to get moving. He washed his face in the cold, cold creek and it made him feel instantly wide-awake. He filled everyone's canteens then woke his fellow robbers. When he thought to call them that it made him cringe and he decided not to refer to them that way no matter how true it was.

"Let's get moving, we are burning daylight," He said. He handed each of them some of dried jerky and biscuits.

"This ain't much to eat but we all will fill our bellies at Dinner Station tonight." The horses were packed and ready to go in less than ten minutes. Even though they were far gone from the bank and had seen no sign of a posse, not a one of the group wanted to be responsible for lagging behind. They all had wives, families, ranches and yes, a certain standing in society. Not a one of them wanted to be caught.

They rode mostly east at a rapid clip for most of the day. They traded the horse they rode for the spare every so often. Even though the horses were in fact traveling, not carrying a man made a difference in their traveling ability.

Near evening they wandered into Dinner Station. Here they bought a place to sleep in the barn and a warm meal. They all thoroughly enjoyed the feeling of food in their stomachs. At this point in their journey they increasingly felt assured that they weren't being followed. And tonight, bedded down in the Dinner Station barn, with full stomachs, they slept well. After two days of little sleep, fast riding and adrenaline pumping through their veins, yes they slept well.

At the rising of the sun, the men took the money from their saddlebags and divided out Green Berry's split. He also added Bige's split to his saddlebags. The men took breakfast at the diner. Green Berry caught the early stage to Elko. His part of the plan was now to meet Bige at the train station and they would take the train home to Texas.

Horseback the men were now three men traveling and anyone who might be looking for the bank robbers would be looking for four. That made them feel somewhat more at ease. It would be good for Bige and Green Berry too.

Tap, Ira and Jim headed north toward Charleston. A few miles south of the town they headed over the big mountain and dropped down into Mary's River. As the horses moved sometimes the gold would make a tinkling sound as it rattled around in the bags. Jim smiled every time he heard it. He loved that sound. This would mean a whole new life a whole new start for him and his darlin' Lizzie.

They camped on Mary's River that night and the next morning they headed up the mountain. The climb up to Hummingbird Springs was steep and at times treacherous. The horses were sweating freely. The men were extra glad for this morning's brisk mountain air. When they reached the top of the mountain, they stopped at the spring to water their horses and to let them rest.

Ira looked down the mountain. What a beautiful sight lay before them. Home. They still had a good 20 miles to make it to Three Creek. Fortunately it would all be downhill and much easier than what they had experienced earlier that day. He sure hoped all was well with Sarah and the kids. He had been gone a long time...physically and mentally. As far as Sarah knew, he was down on the desert running horses again. What she would say when he returned again busted, he wasn't sure. But this he had to do for his brother Levi, and it was almost over.

Before they got to Jim's place they decided to stop at Faraday's place for a celebration drink. There were more people than usual at the store and all the place was buzzing about the ROBBERY. Ira's face paled white. He had just started to feel sure that they had gotten away with it.

"How in the hell do these people know?" He wondered. They ordered their whiskey and sat down. As they drank, Tap asked the man sitting next to him what the noise was all about.

"You aint heard?" He snorted. "Ole man Faraday was robbed in the middle of the night a few days back." This man got more animated as he told the story. "A couple of men held him and his wife up at gunpoint. Scared the dirt right outta him. I hear he now wants to sell out. The men didn't get much money but they took some hats and coats and a lot of food."

Tap smiled and a visible relief washed over his face. All three men enjoyed their whiskey more after that. Pretty soon they figured it was time to be getting on home. Tap would stay a few more days with Jim. The setting sun dictated that Ira would spend one more night with Jim and Tap.

In the morning before he left, Ira looked seriously at Tap. He said, "When you pass through Denver," he paused thinking how to put this..."There was a beautiful blue dress at the dry goods that I meant to buy for Sarah but never did. Could you send it to me?"

Tap studied his face to be sure he understood. "From Denver you mean?" he queried. Then he added, "You have my word, my friend." Then he winked at Ira. Ira then rode off in the early morning light toward his home.

Jim and Tap rested up most of the day. They had been running on nerves and adrenaline for the last few days. Now that they were home they needed to make up for the stress. Lizzie fed them a good dinner and Tap told Jim he had his most ingenious idea ever.

"I know how we can make this Faraday robbery cover our tracks from Winnemucca forever." Jim was listening anxiously. "Cassidy and his Wild Bunch have used my name to cover some of their deeds in the past...This time I am gonna use theirs to cover us. They owe it to me." He smiled.

"Tonight, I am gonna take two of these $100.00 gold pieces and the money sack from the bank. I will leave it at the door to the store with a note."

Around midnight, Jim and Tap snuck up to Faraday's store. The note he nailed to the door read:

Sorry for the scare old timer. We needed the grub and coats and money to get to Winnemucca. Hope this will cover yer trouble. Til we meet again. Butch

Tap nailed the note and the sack to the door. They headed back to Jim's place. Tap chuckled to himself all the way back and every time he thought of it for many days to come. He was so tickled by his ingenious idea.

Jim and Tap snuck up to Faraday's store in the middle of the night. They left the money sack, $200 .00 and a note they hoped would cover their tracks forever from the bank robbery. The note read:

Sorry for the scare old man. We neeeded the grub, coats and the money to get to Winnemucca. Hope this will cover yer trouble. Til we meet again.

Butch

Winnemucca Route
By I + B

Three Dr.

Mountain City

Togot mountain

Charleston Hemming Bird SP

Marys River

30

30

90

Deeth · Wells

Elko

Tuscahon

Willow Db

Dinner Station →

30

Rail Rd

Highway

75

Evans Db

Kimtral

Golconda

↓ 15

Winnemucca

Chapter 12
Ira Returns Home

Ira left Jim and Tap early, anxious but apprehensive to return home. How could he explain convincingly, to Sarah that running horses with Tap was again a bust. Earlier this summer, when they were planning the route to Winnemucca, they had used the excuse that they were gone running horses. Ira had said he had a new horse market possibility and needed new horses to break.

Sarah had cooked up biscuits and made jerky to send. She also sent him some bacon and a bag of coffee and beans. When planning the route down, Tap had been many times with cattle through the O'Neil, to the rail head at Deeth. He thought that this was the route they should take. Ira instead took him south of Jim's and from there up the mountain to Humming Bird Springs. From there they dropped into Mary's River and just kept following the creeks south and east to Winnemucca. Tap agreed that his route saved several travel miles. As they rode along they identified where they would stop and where they would exchange horses. They generally planned the getaway.

When Ira mentioned that he might be a little old for such an undertaking as this Tap told him that the wisdom and wit of old age would trump the agility and enthusiasm of youth any day. If they planned this deed well they would be successful. Ira agreed. If they carefully planned this things would go a lot easier.

When they returned to home, Tap spent several more days with Ira and his family. They were in fact meticulously planning out every detail of this business venture. Sarah wasn't happy when they returned without horses. Actually it was more out of concern for his family than he realized at the time.

Now here he was again short months later in the very same spot. For the next several miles as he rode toward home, he was constructing what he was going to say to her. Before he reached his yard, he saw his sons Bert and Chet and Levi's son Ed coming down the road to meet him. They were anxious to see the new horses he had gathered. He told them that unfortunately he thought the horse herd had been either gathered or had moved on north to the Snake. Bert stood as tall and straight as he could before his dad and told him he thought he could make a hand on the next gather. After all, he was 14 now and nearly grown. Ira ruffled the young man's hair and said he'd have to think that over.

Sarah and Inez were out in the garden picking the last of the vegetables. The September nights were getting cold. A frost was sure to be here soon. Ira walked up behind his pretty wife and gathered her in his arms. He pulled her close to him. She sent the kids out to milk the cow.

"I am glad to see you home Ira." She said. "I missed you and the kids missed you."

"What no horses, again?" She asked. There was a suspicious sounding tone to her voice.

"Not even a sign," He said. "I think they have all moved north to the Snake for permanent."

"Ira," she said, "is.. is it really horses you're a chasing? "

He looked at her for a long time. Finally, he took her hand in his, "You, Sarah are my world. " His eyes got very misty.

"Besides that look at me, Sarah, I am tired and filthy and I think I smell worse than a rattlesnake den." He looked deep into her eyes and said. "No other woman has ever, even turned my head since I met you."

With the look that he gave her, she knew that in this, his pledge of devotion to her, he was telling her the truth.

Satisfied that her marriage was okay, she pulled away from Ira and added, "I really don't want that Tap Duncan hangin' round anymore. I was glad when he left this country and I just wished he would stay gone. He is just bad news and he'll get you...us in trouble, Ira."

With that Ira smiled at her. He said, "I don't look to see Tap in this country much anymore. The wild horse trade seems played out from here. Those Wilkins with the diamond brand seem to be capturing anything that runs for their trade. They are running from Bruneau across the desert and up to Wilkin's Island. As they move from range to range they take it all. Feed and animals. "

She thought on the horses a while then switched her thoughts back to Tap. "Well I hope he doesn't come back, ever!" she said.

Ira settled in at home and got to work taking care of all the things that piled up all summer while he was working on the Winnemucca deal. He thought about how ironic it seemed, when most people thought about a life of crime they often referred to bank robbers and horse thieves as being too lazy to work. Truth be told, Ira had never worked so hard on anything in his life. This deal had consumed his time, resources and abilities. Now he felt an odd sort of accomplishment and the worst part was not being able to talk to anyone about it.

A few weeks later Sarah received a package at the Butte Post Office. She was curious as to who might be sending her something. The package was wrapped in brown paper and tied with a thin leather strap, knotted in the front. A return address read, Tap Duncan, Denver. She looked curiously at Ira, then put the package down. Somehow seeing that it was from Tap, seemed to disgust her. Ira picked it up and said if she wasn't gonna open he would. He too, was curious as to what it might be.

Sarah relented and took the package. She carefully cut the leather that tied it with Ira's knife. Pulling the paper back, she couldn't believe her eyes. There folded up lay a beautiful blue dress, similar to the one she had seen years before at the dry goods store. Sarah's eyes filled with tears. A note lay on top of the dress. She handed that to Ira. It read: "The promise is kept. Tap." Now Ira's eyes filled with tears. Sarah's delight with the dress seemed to change her heart.

She even told Ira that maybe she should change her mind about that Tap Duncan. "He sure knows the way to a woman's heart."

Ira looked at her. "Now wait a moment there sweetheart," he said, "It was my idea that he should send you the dress."

She smiled and held the dress close to her body she said, "Oh Ira, I love it." Ira felt good inside.

In the spring as the snow melted and it was time to take the cattle and the sheep south to the mountain, Jim came to visit. Ira was glad for his company and he accompanied Ira taking cattle to the mountain. It gave them a chance to talk as they rode.

"Faraday's selling the store and Lizzie and I are buying it" Jim said. "Faraday is old and feeble and that robbery last fall took more than his store goods, it took the heart right out of him."

Jim mentioned Tap's note and that Faraday had gotten a lot of attention and fame over being robbed by "Butch." Everyone had assumed that it was Butch Cassidy and the Sundance kid. News had traveled fast to Nixon and to Winnemucca and even to the Wild bunch. Seems that they had sent a picture of themselves to Nixon thanking him for the cash. Jim was impressed by Tap's genius in writing that note and their good fortune.

Ira smiled at those words. "Yeah." he said.

He thought about what Tap's note had meant to him for his brother Levi's sake and what the dress had meant to Sarah. All this past winter it seemed that they shared their best relationship since they married. If he had known how much happiness a new dress would bring her, he would have bought her several more throughout the years.

Jim said Lizzie had gotten a mail contract and they were gonna be in the merchant business. "This really does give you and Lizzie a new lease on life, I am happy for you Jim."

"Yeah," Jim said, "but there is one more thing. I really need your help. Didn't you and your dad build a stone jailhouse back in Colorado?"

"Yeah, now that was a long time ago," Ira replied.

Jim continued. "I want to move the store down the creek to my place," Jim said. "That old log store is gonna burn one of these days and I want to build a sturdy stone store." Jim seemed younger than Ira remembered. Fresh ideas brought him new energy it seemed.

"Would you help me build my store, Ira?" Jim offered to pay well. Both men chuckled at that. The Brackett boys, Bert and Chet were now 12 and 14 and since Levi's son Ed, had come to stay with them, help to tend the home fires was plentiful at least for now so Ira agreed.

Chapter 13
The Texas Filly Comes to Idaho 1911

Ira helped Jim build a good and sturdy store. Since Tap's ingenious note to Faraday it was widely accepted by the strong arm of the law that the Wild Bunch had committed the robbery in Winnemucca. The Pinkerton detective agency added that robbery to the list of debauchery attributed to the Wild Bunch.

And Green Berry, Bige, Jim, Tap and Ira true to their pact never spoke a word of it. All the men returned to life as usual. Their ranches and businesses were prospering and their families were growing.

Last Christmas, Jim had sent a letter to his brother Bige in San Saba. He was so enthused with this new merchant business. In the last few years gold had been discovered just to the south and west and a new boom town called Jarbidge, Nevada had sprung up overnight. He mentioned that the gold strike had grown his business and enterprises substantially and he was looking for some help. Seems that he and Lizzie were overworked and it was taking a toll on their marriage.

When Bige read that Jim needed help it was like this letter was sent from on high. His younger daughter Ora Lee, now 19 years old was a spitfire. She was gorgeous and she loved to have fun. She had been as of late, associating with some young men that Bige considered less than desirable, especially as candidates to be his son-in-law. She had heard about the escapades of her uncles (The Duncans and the Ketchums), and she seemed to feel they had much glamour to their lives. When Bige figured enough thaw had come to Three Creek that spring, he decided to take Ora to Idaho to get her out of Texas. Jim had eagerly decided she would be great help at the store. There was a rail that ran now to Rogerson so they could take the train most of the way there. Bige and Ora were so impressed by the fancy buckboard that Jim drove to pick them up. Ora began warming to the idea of leaving Texas and her friends.

As they were crossing the Salmon, Jim pointed to the north and talked about the dam that was being constructed where the canyon narrowed.

"A reservoir for homesteading farmers downstream." he said

Bige remarked that soon this wild west would be as populated as Texas. As they continued Jim suggested that they stop at Whiskey Slough to see their old friend Ira. Bige eagerly agreed. Ira was so tickled to see his old friends. Especially so as Bige introduced his daughter. Immediately Ira thought to his son Bert and what a striking match these two might make. Ira asked if they planned to stay and Bige said he would be there until after the 4th of July and that Ora would be staying on at Jim and Lizzie's.

The boys, Bert and Chet and Ed were all gone on a horse gathering trip with Tap. Seems that he had just purchased a substantial ranch in Arizona, the Diamond Bar, and was looking to stock it. While there were perhaps closer herds of wild horses, Tap knew this country like the back of his hand and if there were horses available, he knew how to get them. Especially so around Clover Creek where there were some small, dead end box type canyons where a guy could cut a set of horses from the larger herd and slow them long enough to convince them they didn't have to travel with the rest of the herd. In the open desert, young colts could run a man and a horse to death before you could get them settled to head a new direction. Before the turn of the century, catching and breaking these wild horses had been a major part of Tap and Ira's income. It didn't seem quite fair that when the Wilkins moved in they had taken all the horses. When Tap and Ira harvested the wild bunch they took a few but always left some too.

Several people spoke of the horses that still ran free farther north and east all the way along the Snake River from Glenns Ferry to Hagerman. From Arizona, Tap brought up a crew including some of his nephews and he had every intention of taking some of these wild Idaho animals back to his Diamond Bar Ranch. They had stopped by Ira's place for a visit and Tap had invited him along. Ira however had a new enterprise going. He was supplying meat and fruit to the dam builders and he had negotiations to complete. He did however, agree to let his boys go along.

It took two days heading mostly north and west to arrive at the banks of the Snake River. They camped there that night. Chet was amazed at the size of that river. He hadn't known there was that much water in all the state of Idaho. They didn't break camp until the sun was well up that next morning. Tap said this was the waiting part. They did pack their gear and have their horses ready for a later time that morning.

When the sun seemed high, probably near noon, true to the legends that he had heard a massive herd of horses began pouring off the hillside and down to the river to water. It was a beautiful sight.

As a group of horses watered and began making their way up the hillside to graze, Tap and his boys tried to haze a group of them to the west. Tap hoped that the sheer number of them would be enough to convince the horses to head where they wanted them to go. Without a natural corral Tap had realized this was a gamble but he was willing to try. They would just start to get a group headed to run fast and hard. And just as they would think they had them, the colts would bust away with the mares following close behind. They would head in all directions. As one cowboy would break out to bring a horse back, another would bust back. The riders tried all day to get some horses headed out. It seemed as if the horses had a plan: scatter if they try to catch you.

After a few days of this failure Tap finally called the boys off and they set camp for the night. That evening a few men rode up to their camp. They too had been running horses and were headed back to Bruneau. One man recognized Tap.

Tap originally hadn't planned to spend much time in this country and now a man from these parts had seen him. He didn't want anyone to know he was in these parts especially not the kin of the man he had shot. He made the hard decision that he needed to get on south away from this country. They traveled that day back toward Clover Creek. Tap was not happy. He needed horses for his ranch but needed to stay alive more. That night they camped in one of those box type canyons.

Early the next morning, Tap woke to the sound of horses' hooves in the camp. Panicked he rose thinking that their horses had escaped the lariat corral his men had set. Tap pulled his boots on and ran over to the man who was night watch for the mounts. The horses were ok. Seems that sometime during the night, they had drawn in a herd of horses traveling the desert.

The dawning of the sun colored the sky just pink enough for him to make out the shadows of about 200 head of horses. Tap began to chuckle.

"If I was a praying man, I would just have to say thank you." Tap woke his men. He told them quietly but quickly saddle up. His plan was to make a circle north of the horses. Because they would take the whole of this herd they could avoid the horse races and busts of the previous days. They would need a couple of their fastest and most agile cowboys in the lead to keep the leaders headed south and the rest would form a corral to follow up behind.

Tap's men were mounted and ready to go in mere minutes. The excitement of finding these horses fueled their hopes especially since just yesterday, the thought returning to Arizona busted was a real possibility. The cowboys surrounded the herd and headed them south and east.

As the sun began to light the desert, Tap began to realize that these horses carried a brand. A diamond in fact. How easily they would fit in at the diamond bar he smiled. Tap didn't say anything to his crew. They just kept moving. Tap began to think about how he and Ira had gathered horses here on this very desert. Those horses that they gathered broke and sold were sometimes the difference in lean and prosperous years. They never took more of the horse herd than they needed or could put to good use, leaving some for others and seed for the next year. When Wilkins began sweeping the desert clean as they moved their herd Tap and Ira both had find ways to make up for the lost income in those years.

Tap kept the herd moving as quickly as he could. By the time the herd reached the big corrals at Smith's Crossing on Big Flat Creek, night was settling in. There the crew and the horses spent the night. Early the next morning they headed the horses east until they hit the big springs at the head of Antelope Creek. The herd was traveling fast and every so often, one of the younger cowboys would rope a new mount and break him to ride simply and buck him out and get him ready to carry another cowboy. It would be a long trip back to Arizona and they would need a lot of fresh fast horses to keep up with this herd.

Near Whiskey Slough, Bert, Chet and Ed headed for home. Tap promised to send them their pay from his Diamond Bar Ranch in Arizona when he returned. Bert said he guessed the money would be great but honestly for him this trip was the most fun he had ever had. With a chuckle, Tap and his men headed south, across the Salmon, past the San Jacinto and the Boar's Nest. Always south, these horses were headed to Arizona.

Chet, however, was more than a little confused. He could read a brand too. He knew those horses weren't wild. He had just participated in horse thievery. "I think they hang guys for that!" He thought. They had just stolen thousands of dollars in horse flesh and now Tap wants to send us a week's worth of cowboy's wages. Chet was disgusted thoroughly. Through family legends he had heard of Tap and he knew his mom didn't like him. Now he knew for himself what a rascal he was.

At home, Ira was glad to see his boys. He had in fact missed their help. A few weeks later he announced to them that there would be a family vacation this year. Things were looking good. The contract had been signed and he was selling beef and fruit to the dam builders and at a good price too. Years ago, when Sarah sent to Colorado to get those trees, Ira thought that she had gotten too many. She spent so many hours laboring over them, pruning, watering and harvesting and canning. This year he would have to apologize to her. Their fruit was worth twice as much as his beef. The men building the dam would buy all the fruit he could produce. They had given Ira 16 cents a pound for the plums and they would receive only 8 cents a pound for his beef. The spring had been wet and without frost. Things looked good for a bumper crop.

There was to be in the new boomtown of Jarbidge a huge Fourth of July celebration. Back in Denver there had always been a celebration for the nation's birth. Ira was glad to be able to take his family to attend a celebration. It would be their first ever. Jim and Lizzie and their pretty niece from Texas would be there too.

Chapter 14
The Fourth of July

Ora Lee had settled in at her Uncle Jim and Aunt Lizzie's place. She was surprised at how well she liked the store. With the mining activity at Jarbidge there was a constant stream of customers at their establishment. Actually there was more interaction with people than she had ever had in Texas. And at this time in her life that was something she enjoyed. The weather here was cooler than in Texas and that too suited her just fine. She kept busy helping Lizzie sort mail and they had even begun serving some meals. Bige, her dad, and Uncle Jim were really enjoying their time together. They were working on building a new horse corral behind the store.

In late June, Jim announced that the store was to be closed for a couple days the first part of July. There was to be a huge celebration in the boom town of Jarbidge and they would travel there and be a part of it. Ora was so excited. She had watched the young men who stopped at the store on their way through to Jarbidge. There were definitely a few she wouldn't mind seeing again.

She spent the next few days sorting through her clothes trying to decide on just the right dress to wear. The morning came to head south to Jarbidge. Jim loaded up in the buckboard. They took bed rolls. They would be camping out. Most of Jarbidge lived in tents. Buildings had been built but land was scarce and there would not be rooms to rent. The drive over the island was like nothing Ora had ever experienced ever. This country sure wasn't Texas. In Jarbidge, they pulled up to a spot just north of town and decided to make camp. Late afternoon was now upon them and the barbeque would start soon.

Lizzie helped Ora lace her corset and get her dress on. Just up the canyon from their camp, another young lady Ora had befriended at Three Creek was camped. Ora asked if it was ok if she went to find Vada, her friend. She promised to meet up with her kin at the barbeque later. She was glad when the sun began to set low against the canyon walls and the air began to cool. Sporting a dress wasn't entirely to her liking but for such an occasion as this it was entirely appropriate. She soon found her friend and the short walk to the bustling town was a lot more fun in the company of another young lady. They watched handsome young cowboys as they traveled the streets and young children as they played. The food at the barbeque was great.

As the sun light completely faded, several bonfires burned in the streets and lanterns were lit outside the buildings and the tents lining the main street. A band struck up and Ora made the comment that she would like to hear the more bluegrass type of music from her home. Vada told her to wait. As soon as one band tired another would strike up. A street dance was in full swing. Suddenly Vada stopped what she was saying.

"There he is." she whispered excitedly. She grabbed Ora's arm. " I look okay, right?" She asked.

Vada had seen this young man on various occasions in Three Creek and thought he was the most handsome guy she had ever seen. Ora looked at him curiously. He was indeed handsome but standing next to him was the cowboy who caught her eye.

"Vada" she said. "You can have him," her voice trailed off, "but that one's mine," as she said that she pointed at Bert.

About that time the cowboys saw her gesture their way. The girls were a little embarrassed but they smiled sweetly.

"They are coming over here." Ora said.

Vada's young man did ask her to dance and that left Ora and Bert alone. Bert seemed to fumble over his words. He wasn't sure if he should take his hat off when he spoke to her. Finally he just took a deep breath and asked her to dance. They danced and they danced some more.

When Ora told him that she was from Texas he asked if she knew Jim and Lizzie Duncan. Their conversation began to roll from there. They spoke of common interests and common people, and pretty soon they were talking as if they had grown up together. He told her about running horses with her Uncle Tap only weeks before and that he had met her brother Loys Boy on the gather. He left out the stealing the horses part, hoping she would know. After the fireworks show, Bert walked Ora back to her campsite. She shivered in the cool mountain air and Bert quickly took his own coat off and placed it around her shoulders.

"You are quite the gentleman, aren't you Bert Brackett." He liked the way she said his name and the teasing in her voice.

They could have kept on talking 'til the sun rose again but that just wouldn't have been appropriate. Agreeing to meet for breakfast the next morning, Bert left for his own campsite. Jim, Lizzie and Bige could see the huge smile on her face even in the campfire glow.

The next morning their camps were pulled early. Ora had met Bert at the breakfast and he had asked her to accompany him in his buckboard back to Three Creek. Last night when he returned to camp he told his dad that he had met a beautiful young lady and she was staying with Jim and Lizzie Duncan. She was helping at the store and oh was she beautiful. Bert wondered if he could take the wagon and the fancy black team and escort her to her home. Ira smiled when he remembered meeting this Ora. She was beautiful and he had immediately matched her with his son. Without mentioning that thought they seemed to be on the same path.

So Bert drove up to Ora's camp with the fanciest set of black horses she had ever seen. Ira's one indulgence was that he drove fancy wagons with even fancier high stepping horses. The two young folk headed up and over the top of Wilkin's Island and on over to Three Creek. Ora was impressed with the gentle but strong way he handled the reins and the horses. The horses seemed to understand his commands and respond quickly. The trip to the store seemed to end all too quickly. Bert helped her carry her things to the house and then just seemed to linger a little longer. He liked the sweet way she smelled. Soon Ira and the rest of the family pulled up. He told Bert they had best get a move on to make it home by night fall. He asked Ora when he could see her again. She just smiled and said, "Soon I hope."

Jim and his crew arrived shortly afterward. Bige needed to catch the train tomorrow to return to Texas so after dinner that night he asked Ora to go walking with him. He asked her if she would like to stay on in this country.

"I would like that very much, Pa" she said.

She smiled warmly. Bige had seen that look on his own Nancy Blake's face before they married and on the faces of the other girls as their time for love had come.

There was an uneasy silence then she swallowed hard and said, "I, uh I think he's the one Pa."

Bige stopped short. She had only met this fellow days before. True, he himself liked the idea of having them together but marriage, and so quickly?

"I'm gonna have to talk to that young man then." he said.

Ora grabbed her father's arm "Uhh you can't do that. Pa. He, he doesn't know we are getting married...yet anyway."

Bige laughed. "My dear beautiful Ora you have always been strong willed and what you have wanted you have gotten. Maybe, I should warn him before I leave!" He laughed and so did she.

He pulled her tight and hugged her.

"I am happy for you baby but I am sure gonna miss you." The cracking of his voice made tears come to her eyes. He continued. " I worry about leaving you here but with your Uncle Jim well you are blood and he always cares for his own, and from what you are telling me now, you'll be alright. However." he stopped and pulled something out of his coat pocket. "I want you to have this," he said. He handed her a small carry pistol nestled in a leather sheath.

"What with coyotes and rattlesnakes both the human and the animal kind, a pretty girl like you needs an equalizer." He swallowed hard like he was trying to fight back the tears. "Hope you never have to use it."

Ora hugged him. "I will be okay Pa, but I am sure gonna miss you."

Chapter 15
Courting the Texas Filly

It had been nearly a week since the 4th of July and Bert had been busy helping his father at the ranch. Some of the fruit had already begun to ripen and had to be picked and delivered to the dam site. When the last of the first crop was delivered he asked his father if he could take the fancy buck board and go to Three Creek on Sunday. Ira knew he shouldn't ask why but couldn't resist seeing his son blush.

Truthfully, Ira had wondered if the romance was off but he could quickly see by Bert's reaction that it was still hot. When Saturday night bath time came around Chet thought that Bert spent longer than usual getting clean When Chet teased him about getting all clean for a girl he just told him he wished he was so lucky.   Chet very truthfully thought "Yeah, you are right."

Ira got up early the next morning to help Bert hitch up the black team. When Bert arrived at the store, Ora was surprised, pleasantly, to see him.

"Beginning to think you'd forgotten me Bert Brackett." she smiled.

He took is hat off his head trying to remember his manners. Holding it to his chest he asked her to go riding with him. She glanced at the chores she needed to finish and then to her Aunt Lizzie. Fond of young love herself, Lizzie told her to go but to pack a picnic from the kitchen. They rode in the wagon looking for a good spot to share that picnic. It didn't take Bert a week before the next time he came to call on his pretty Texas filly.

Later that fall, they attended several dances at Rogerson. After one dance, as Bert was driving her home, they were quietly riding along listening to the clop of the horses' hooves as they pulled along. Bert pulled the horses up.

He looked at her and said, "You know Ora, you'd do a lot better coming home with me and raising kids and horses than sorting mail and selling groceries."

She looked at him for a long time. Then she began, "Not until after you ask me to marry you Bert."

Bert was fumbling so terribly with his words. He was holding his hat to his chest, he looked so humble. He swallowed hard and said, "I thought that was what I was asking you, Ora."

She smiled. "Oh," she said.

Wherever you go
I will go,
wherever you lodge
I will lodge.

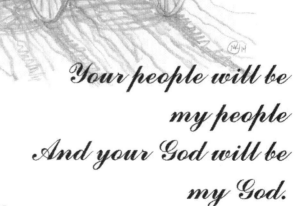

Your people will be
my people
And your God will be
my God.

Ruth 1:16

He waited for more of a response and didn't get one, so he gigged up the team and drove on. He felt so bad, he wanted this to be just right and he was sure he had messed it up. The horses traveled on about a mile or so. Ora then knew she had waited long enough she thought she saw his striking blue eyes begin to tear up. I better respond she thought, before he changes his mind. Ora then reached up and put her soft hand on his as he held the reins.

She looked at him, "Okay," she smiled, "Okay."

When Bert returned home that day he met his father at the Cedar Creek. From the smile on the young man's face his dad knew this hadn't been just an ordinary dance. Bert told him what he had been feeling for Ora and how he felt bad that courting her had taken so much of his time.

"It's like this unseen force is just drawing me to her, Dad, I think about her all the time."

Ira smiled at Bert's words. He thought back to his courtship days with that lovely Miss Sarah when his colts seemed of their own accord to travel by the Mauldin place. And Ira told him as much.

"Dad," he said. "I asked her to marry me." This time those blue, blue eyes of Bert's did fill with tears. But so did those of Ira.

"Well son, this is a good start."

Through the next months as the wedding plans were made, Ira told Bert that since he and Sarah were spending more time at Cedar Creek, Whiskey Slough should make a good home for the newlyweds. A few days later when Bert was at the Three Creek store to pick up Ora for a date, he was waiting outside for her. He began looking at the outside of the store and he marveled at how well the stones were fitted together. It occurred to him that Ira had built this stone store using the stone mason skills that he learned from Grandpa Ozro. Bert remarked to himself that the store seemed put together more solidly than any building he had ever seen. Then a thought came to him, sort of like a whisper from on high from his grandpa.

"Build a house for her." He felt those words more than heard them.

Bert was filled with emotion. He had to quickly compose himself when she came out the door.

"Let's go riding," she smiled and hopped in the wagon seat.

When Bert returned home he stopped off to see his dad first. He found him out feeding.

"Dad," Bert began, "I uh I want to build a good solid house for a good solid marriage." He blurted it out quickly so he wouldn't change his mind.

"You were always the most sentimental of the kids, you know." His father said.

Bert explained what had happened earlier that day at the store and what he had felt. As he heard the story, Ira knew that he had no choice but to help Bert build a house.

"Your grandpa wants us to do this," he said.

A few days later they all met at Whiskey Slough and picked a place close to the fruit trees that Sarah had planted years before. Father and son worked together on constructing a solid rock home. Ira decided that if they put a lot of time and effort on this project, it could be a honeymoon home for his son and new daughter-in-law come the third of February.

Chapter 16
Tick Fever

With Bert and Ora starting a family and living at Whiskey Slough, Ira and Sarah settled into their lives at Cedar Creek. He continued running sheep and cattle up on the mountain to the south of them. Even though he was getting on in age, he still enjoyed working with wild horses. He would do much of the ground work but depended on Chet and Bert to do much of the riding. It was still a matter of pride with him that he have the best looking team in the country.

About 1919 word came to Ira that a reputable sheep breeder from Montana was coming to town. Because he was constantly on the lookout for ways to improve his herds and flocks he hitched up his team and drove to Rogerson. The train the sheep man was riding in on was late so Ira busied himself buying the supplies he needed for the ranch. Ira determined he wanted to meet with the sheep man. The train did arrive later and Ira got a good look at the information on this new blood line. Ira was eager to add some of that blood to his flock. Ira agreed to buy a couple rams and a few ewes. They shook on the deal and the sheep man departed.

Upon leaving the hotel, Ira was a bit concerned at the lateness of the afternoon. His concern grew deeper when about Antelope Springs the rain began to fall. He had his usual high stepping black geldings that ate up the miles so he was sure he'd make it home before too much storm settled in. But as the wind blew and the thunder began to roll around him he was not sure he would beat the storm. By now the occasional flash of lightening seemed to strike ever closer to him, At the gate about a quarter mile from home, he pulled the team up, carefully tied the reins to the wagon brake handle and got off the wagon to open it up. He opened the gate and walked back toward the wagon. A huge flash of lightning struck the fence not 20 yards away and the thunder clapped as quickly almost as he saw the flash. The team already skittish from the now nighttime blackness, spooked and bolted forward knocking him to the ground. As they did they drug the heavily loaded wagon over his leg. The wagon headed down the road and to the house. He lay there in the mud and rain for a few moments. He began to shiver.

"I guess I am still alive," he said out loud.

As he tried to get up his one leg gave way underneath him. He then realized that he was in a bad way. At first he thought to wait until morning when someone would see his renegade team and come looking for him. But as he lay there in the cold wet rain and the even colder mud, he realized that he probably wouldn't last that long. He decided there was nothing other to do than to crawl back to the house. Crawling on the ground soaked him to the bone. But between the shock of breaking his leg and the tremendous exertion it required to pull his body closer to his home, he thought he was warm.

At long last he made it. Their old cow dog Jack, growled and barked warningly until he decided it was Ira out there in the dark. He crawled up on the porch and began banging on the door. Sarah and Chet both came out. They immediately drug him in the house and cleaned him up. They put dry clothes on his except for his pants. Chet headed to Rogerson to fetch the doctor. Even though he did reset that leg, it never healed properly and he never really recovered.

The sheep did arrive and in the spring Ira and Chet were working them. Ira was excited to see how the new lamb crop would be. A few days later, while they were out choring, Ira excused himself from the corrals. He said he really needed to go lay down for just a little while. Chet noticed that his dad's hands and arm were red and spotted but he thought it was just from working in the cold of the spring day.

That evening, Sarah realized that there was more wrong with her husband than just being tired. He had a terrible rash on his hands and feet and it was growing up his extremities. For all that night she sat up with him. She put a wet cloth on his forehead to try to break his fever. In the morning, Chet took a fast horse and again headed to Rogerson to fetch the doctor.

When the doctor arrived, he took one look at Ira and knew that he had Rocky Mountain Spotted Fever. Recently he attended a conference talking about this disease, this tick fever. It was most common in the sheep country of Montana and he wondered if Ira had maybe been there.

"No," Sarah replied, but he recently got some sheep from there.

The doctor said that unfortunately there wasn't a cure yet for this sort of thing. Ira could recover but most likely it would be just a matter of days before he died. Sarah felt so sick inside. What would she do without her Ira. They had lived so much life together and what an adventure it had been. Yes, the boys now grown men would be able to manage the ranch but for her personally, how could she live without him, her anchor in life. The doctor gave him some medicine mostly a pain killer to try to make him comfortable. He said that whiskey might be better. He would give them all the help he could.

The next few days, Ira slept some but mostly just want Chet to sit with him. Sarah tried to keep herself busy with her house work and chores. She left Chet to try to keep his father comfortable. He would give him the whiskey when the he would ball up in pain. As they sat Chet told his dad that he had something that he wanted to get off his chest.

Ira said "Well, we're a talkin', let's have it."

Chet asked him to recall when they sold the fruit to the dam builders then he continued, "You were busy but let us boys go with Tap to round up horses you remember?" Chet swallowed hard.

"I, uhh...we helped him steal a bunch of branded horses, Wilkin's horses," Chet blurted it out quickly before got scared and he changed his mind. He hated keeping that secret. In the first place it was something that he wasn't willingly in on. Chet was scared of what his dad might say but he felt surprisingly good, like a huge burden was lifting off his shoulders.

Ira, seeing his son's sadness patted his son's leg with his feeble spotted hand. He seemed lost in his own thoughts for a long time, actually long enough that Chet was afraid his father hadn't heard him or that the shock of Chet stealing horses finished him off. Then Ira cleared his throat, he took a very long sip from the whiskey bottle and sighed.

"Son," he smiled, "Now I have a thing or two to tell you about Tap Duncan!"

Ira spoke of leaving Denver and the fear he felt for his family. When he came to the part, later about the bank robbery in Winnemucca, he made Chet promise to carry that secret to his grave.

"Your mother doesn't know and she can't EVER! You hear me? I want her to still love me even after I die." He got real sad and added, "Keeping these things from her has been hard on me, hard on our marriage."

"Son," he said, "I have tried to do things straight." He paused. "I wouldn't take the money from that robbery, but Tap made me an offer worth more to me than gold."

Chet tried not to show the shock on his face as his father told him that Tap had cleaned up the streets of Arvada. That was his price for handling the getaway horses. Chet thought on his own brother and all the siblings that the family had called their own. His mom's siblings, his uncle Levi's kids and Inez's kids and Bert's too but they didn't live with them.

The tales of Ira's contact with that Tap Duncan made simple horse theft seem like child's play. He wondered if it was the whiskey or maybe the fever that loosened his dad's tongue, but either way, it truly was no wonder that his mom didn't want that Tap hanging around. Chet knew how much better he felt after telling his dad his secret about stealing those horses, he hoped his dad felt better after telling him about his.

Chet sat at his father's side for the next few days. When visitors came to call he would leave his father's side long enough to let them visit but would then return. He never tired of hearing his father's tales of life, a grand life lived.

Somewhere in the night on the 28th of March, dad just silently slipped away. At another time in his life a simple tick bite might have caused him to feel sick, but because his system was weakened by trying to heal from his broken leg, the chill and stress he suffered from the crawl, the bite this time was deadly. He was the first known to succumb to this disease in this part of the country.

Chapter 17
Frank asks for Inez's Hand

Chapter 18
Death Bed Promises Kept

Chapter 19
Settling the Estate

Chapter 20
A Start in Life's Game

Chapter 21
Chet's Musings on Marriage

It was a long winter night in 1960. He took out his pencil and the journal that contained so much of his life. This was what he did on those long lonely nights. He lit the lamp and he wrote. He again began...

As I look back, I can see there are two kinds of marriages. One like my folks had, a true lifelong love affair. No matter what happened at the end of the day, they shared life and love together. I got a close up look what their lives might have been, as they were younger, when I saw Bert and Ora.

They teased each other and were the best of friends. My brother, a bit shy and not saying much for the most part, Ora teasing and flirting some, yet they both knew, there was no one else for them. They had found their life long companion. No matter what happened in life, as long as they had each other, all would be okay. As I watched them, I too, wanted that kind of life and love.

Then there was the other kind of marriage, no matter what one of them did, it wasn't right. Always it could have been, should have been better. To be trapped with one of those hellcats would have been indeed purgatory. If I had to chance that, Chet mused, it was better that I lived alone. Watching Bert and Ora made me think that marriage was for me.

It was the fall of 1919. I thought that things were going well on the ranch and I had some time. I started attending some socials and dances around the country. Down at Buhl, I started seeing this one good-looking girl at most of the socials. I got myself introduced to her so as not to seem too forward. When she spoke her name it was like the sound of angel bells tinkling in my ears. Conversation with her seemed to come so easily. I don't really remember what we talked about, but at each social it seemed like we just spent the whole time visiting.

I told her about the ranch and how Bert had built Ora a honeymoon home and now they had a couple of the cutest kids. She said that sounded like a good life. She had always dreamed of living on a ranch and ranch out in the country. We talked about marriage and what life together would be like. While we did not have solid wedding plans, we talked a lot about the future, our future.

That spring, Dad got sick and died. Bert and Ora were off running their ranch. Frank and Inez were off running and growing an operation of their own. This left the responsibility of running our ranch to me. Mom did a lot but she was pretty broke up. Seems that some days, all she could do was get up and stare out the window waiting for dad to come home.

Truman and Edna were spending a lot of their time with us. In some way it was good, but they still needed lots of time and attention too. They needed us and it certainly wasn't the first time that mom had taken in family members who needed the safety or love of her home.

I found out that just because you are a Brackett, it don't mean you have money. Dad had invested in a ranch that I hadn't known about. It had taken quite a bit of money. He had also invested in one of the mines in Jarbidge before it went bust. All of these things added up. The ranch, though it had lots of livestock and land, it had a lot of debt too. It seemed there weren't enough hours in the day nor days in the week to get everything done that needed done.

One day I woke up and realized that since the spring, I had only seen Miss Emily three times and the last was about 6 weeks ago. There was a social coming up and I determined to go and make up for having neglected her. When I walked in to the dance hall, my heart jumped. There she was and did she look beautiful. My heart sunk however when I saw standing next to her the dirt farmer had always tried to cut in on us. Shyly, I went over near her to say hello. She seemed a bit miffed but she told her dirt farmer to go get her something to drink, she needed to talk to me. When I tried to tell her how I missed her, she said she had missed me too. But while I had been so long gone, she had become engaged. She was getting married. My heart hurt.

"What about us?" I asked. "Our life and the new home we were gonna build at the ranch?"

She said she loved me and probably always would but a girl has to have more than dreams, she's gotta have reality, something solid. She needed something to actually build her life on. She told me that it was the hardest choice she had ever had to make but she had made it.

Then she cradled my face in her soft hands, "Please, don't make this harder on me than it already is."

With that she turned and walked away. She walked over to her dirt farmer, kissed him lightly and said, "Let's go." I was too shocked to do or say anything. My world was walking away. In a daze I stumbled out in to the blackness of the night. I returned to the ranch and dug back into the needed work.

As time went on, I tried to find another fiancée. Every time I met someone and said this might be the one, I went home and looked at Miss Emily's picture on the wall. No, this new girl, I would decide didn't come close to comparing. I would then decide to keep looking. I'd rather not have anyone than have a marriage like some of those around me.

As the years went by, I found myself looking at the girls less and less and talking to Miss Emily's picture more and more.

Closing

Well it is time for me to get moving. As life unfolded Truman and Edna, even though they were Inez's kids became like the kids I never had. I spent a lot of time with them, a lot more than I got to spend with Noy or Beth. Ora was a good mother and she kept them on a short leash. Not that she kept them from me, just that she kept them close.

Now Edna is having a hard time. I think maybe I need her and she needs me. In many respects, she is the daughter I never had. I wish that things had gone better for her, I have tried to help her from time to time. It seems that nothing ever works out right for her. I think I am gonna go down and live with her. I am tired of living alone.

In closing this writing, I have to say that the long winter's nights give a person a lot of time to reflect on life.

The could have dones.

The should have dones.

And more regrettably…

The what ifs.

Much of this was shared with me by my mother or my father. Some of it they said they never shared with anyone else. Some of it is just my observation. Don't know if I should share some of these things with anyone. I'm getting ready to go live at Edna's and if I take this journal, someone may read it and start asking questions. Feelings may get hurt and people may be mad at me. I just don't need any troubles in my life at this time. Still some of this family history some folks should know someday. Maybe 50 years from now. I will stick it up in the attic and someday someone might find it.

I still miss my Miss Emily and I think of the life we could have had.

Editor's Epilogue

We took Uncle Chet's journal and tried to stay true to what he wrote. Some of the original journal entries rambled and repeated themselves. We felt that our family deserved to get the chance to read this and compare the facts according to Uncle Chet with different family stories that they may have heard throughout the years.

We cannot attest to the truthfulness of these reflections other that this is how Uncle Chet wrote them down. And just as some stories were too fresh for him to share during his lifetime; some are too fresh for us to share today. The other chapters in the journal we mentioned by title only and we plan to print them in another 50 years when events are softened by time.

God Bless you all!!! and we look forward to seeing you in 50!

Chet and Kim Brackett

Abijah E. Duncan Sr. was an early West Texas settler and father of four sons, Abijah (Bige) Jr., Richard (Dick) who was hung in Eagle Pass, Texas, James P. (Jim) and George Taplin (Tap).

Abijah E. Duncan Jr.

Married Nancy Blake Ketchum, sister of Green Berry, Tom and Sam Ketchum.

Their daughter was Ora Lee Duncan.

Ora Lee married Bert Brackett, son of Ira Brackett.

James P. (Jim) Duncan

Cowboyed in Texas and New Mexico.

Came to Idaho with his brother Tap in 1892.

Later married Lizzie Helsley and built the rock store at Three Creek.

They later divorced and he moved to Kingman, Arizona with his brother Tap.

Tap Duncan

Cowboyed in Texas and New Mexico.

Married Ollie Binnion in Texas. Came to Idaho with his wife and brother Jim in 1892.

Settled in Three Creek near his friend Ira Brackett. Later he left Idaho to Tanch in Arizona.

Green Berry Ketchum

His sister Nancy Blake married Bige Duncan, Jr.

Their daughter Ora Lee Duncan married Bert Brackett.

Brother-in-law to Bige, Jim, and Tap Duncan and neighbors in Texas and were trading partners.

Ira Brackett

His son Bert married Ora Lee Duncan.

First met the Duncan and Ketchum's at Cherry Creek, Colorado in 1884 when they came through trading horses.

Later Tap and Jim came to Idaho and were neighbors to him.

1812	Ozro Brackett	Born Oct. 22
1849	Ozro Brackett	Married Harriette Blackstone
1850	Green Berry Ketchum jr	Born Oct. 24
1850	Levi Brackett	Born Dec. 28
1852	Ira Brackett	Born Feb. 26 Wisconsin
1853	Harriette Blackstone	Died
1854	Sam Ketchum	Born Jan. 4
1855	Ozro Brackett/Lucy Stone	Married
1856	Abijah Elum Duncan jr	Born Nov 20 Texas son of Abijah E Duncan sr
1859	Ira Brackett and family	left for Colorado
1859	Samuel Brackett	left for Colorado
1862	Jim Duncan	Born Feb 17 son of Abijah E Duncan sr
1862	Sarah Elizabeth Mauldin	Born Jan. 10
1863	Ozro's daughter kidnapped	by Indians
1863	Tom Ketchum	Born Oct 31
1864	Miles Mauldin	Colorado 3rd cavalry
1864	Ozro Brackett	Colorado 3rd cavalry
1864	Richard Dick Duncan	Born Feb 7 son of Abijah E Duncan sr
1865	Ozro Brackett	Builds Franktown jail teaches Ira stone mason skills
1869	Tap Duncan	Born Feb. 4 George Taplin Duncan
1870	Con Shea	Brought Texas cattle to Silver City Idaho

1871	Miles Mauldin	Dies shot by sister in law
1879	Wilkins Family	Moved to Bruneau /horse empire
1880	Ira Brackett/Sarah Mauldin	Married Feb.1
1882	Earl Clark Brackett	Born to Ira and Sarah dies
1884	Frank Clark	Born Oct. 17 marries Inez
1884	Inez Brackett Brackett	Born to Ira and Sarah Jan 9 Mary Inez
1884	Rattlesnake Junction	Became Mountain Home Idaho
1885	Tap Duncan	trail herd to New Mexico Age 16
1886	Bert Brackett	Born Aug 19 Big Flat Creek
1886	Ira Brackett	Comes to Idaho
1888	Chet Brackett Area	My great uncle born Oct 1 Three Creek
1888	Levi Brackett of Ira	Murdered Arvada Colorado Oct 6 brother
1888	Ozro Brackett	Feeling of family trouble
1889	Ozro Brackett	Died Franktown Col Sept 22
1889	Williamson family	Murdered Eagle Pass Texas
1891	Ora Lee Duncan Nancy Blake Ketchum	Born March 1 Abijah Jr Duncan/
1891	Richard Dick Duncan family Sept 18	Hung for murder of Williamson
1891	Tap Duncan	Married Ollie Binnion
1892	Tap Duncan	Moved to Idaho
1894	Tap Duncan	Killed man in Bruneau Bar Oct 16
1898	Tap Duncan	Left Idaho for Arizona

1899	Sam Ketchum	July 24 hung in Santa Fe New Mexico
1900	Abijah Elum Duncan jr	Robbed Winnemucca Bank Sept 19
1900	Green Berry Ketchum jr	Robbed Winnemucca Bank Sep 19
1900	Ira Brackett	Robbed Winnemucca Bank Sept 19
1900	Jim Duncan	Robbed Winnemucca Bank Sept 19
1901	Jim Duncan	Builds Three Creek Store
1901	Tom Ketchum	April 26 Black Jack Ketchum was hung
1904	Tap Duncan	Purchased diamond bar ranch in Arizona
1904	Twin Falls	Plat of town created
1905	TwinFalls	Railway from Shoshone built
1909	Inez Brackett/Frank Clark	Married Jan 6
1909	Jarbidge	Gold discovered in Jarbidge Nev
1910	Rogerson	Railway from Twin Falls built
1911	Bert Brackett	Meets Ora Duncan
1911	Bert Brackett/ Ira honeymoon home	Build rock house Whiskey Slough
1911	Ora Lee Duncan	Comes to Idaho
1911	Truman Clark	Born Inez/Frank Clark
1912	Bert Brackett/ Ora Duncan	Married Feb 3
1913	Edna Clark	Born daughter Inez/ Frank Clark
1913	Noy Brackett	Born Sept 11 son of Bert/Ora Brackett
1914	Green Berry Ketchum jr	Died March 31
1915	Abijah Elum Duncan jr	Died June 27/ Ora Brackett dad

1920	Ira Brackett	Died March 28 Roseworth Idaho
1920	Ira Brackett	Chet death bed promise
1934	Bert Brackett	Died
1934	Sarah Brackett	Died
1972	Chet Brackett	Died	Uncle Chet

Family Group Record

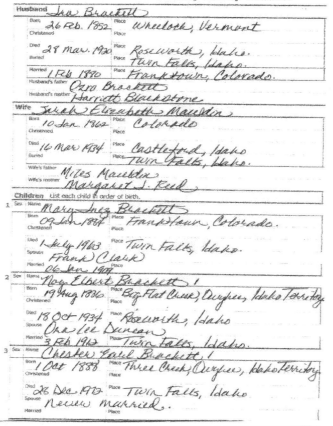

Husband _Ira Brackett_

Born	26 Feb. 1852	Place Wheelock, Vermont
Christened		Place
Died	29 Mar. 1920	Place Roseworth, Idaho.
Buried		Place Twin Falls, Idaho.
Married	1 Feb 1890	Place Franktown, Colorado.
Husband's father	Ozro Brackett	
Husband's mother	Harriett Blackstone	

Wife _Sarah Elizabeth Mauldin_

Born	10 Jan. 1862	Place Colorado
Christened		Place
Died	16 Mar 1934	Place Castleford, Idaho
Buried		Place Twin Falls, Idaho.
Wife's father	Miles Mauldin	
Wife's mother	Margaret J. Reed	

Children List each child in order of birth.

1 Sex: Name _Mary Inez Brackett_

Born	09 Jan 1884	Place Franktown, Colorado.
Christened		Place
Died	1 July 1963	Place Twin Falls, Idaho.
Spouse	Frank Clark	
Married	26 Jan 1909	Place

2 Sex: Name _Roy Elbert Brackett_ /

Born	19 Aug 1886	Place Big Flat Creek, Owyhee, Idaho Territory
Christened		Place
Died	18 Oct 1934	Place Roseworth, Idaho
Spouse	Ona Lee Duncan	
Married	3 Feb 1912	Place Twin Falls, Idaho.

3 Sex: Name _Chester Earl Brackett_ /

Born	1 Oct 1888	Place Three Creek, Owyhee, Idaho Territory
Christened		Place
Died	26 Dec 1972	Place Twin Falls, Idaho
Spouse	never married.	
Married		Place

Ora Lee Duncan
Born March 1, 1891 Knickerbocker, Texas
Died Oct. 11, 1966 Twin Falls, Idaho
    Married Noy Ebert (Bert) Brackett
Born Aug. 19, 1886. Three Creek, Idaho
Died Oct 8, 1934. Twin Falls, Idaho
They were married Feb. 3, 1912 in
Twin Falls, Idaho. They had two children.
1. Noy Ebert (Noy) Brackett
        Born Sept. 11, 1913, Twin Falls, Idaho
2. Mildred Elizabeth (Beth) Brackett
        Born Sept. 20, 1915 Twin Falls, Idaho
                                    d. Sept. 10, 1980 in Twin Falls.
    Noy married Ruby Johnson, born Aug 17, 1919
    b. Pleasant Grove, Utah. They were married
    March 16, 1940. They had six children
1. Ann Lee Brackett, Born April 11, 1941. Twin Falls, Idaho
2. Ellen Jean   "   Born Sept. 19, 1943   "   "   "
3. Eleanor Jean   "   Born Sept. 19, 1943   "   "   "
4. Noy Ebert   " III Born Oct. 17, 1944   "   "   "
5. Ricky Jo   "   Born Jan. 1, 1946   "   "   "
6. Chester Earl   "   Born Jan. 27, 1948   "   "   "

    Beth married Rollick Karl Patrick, born
April 22, 1916. They were married May 27, 1939
in Hailey, Idaho. They had three children
1. Ronda K Patrick, Born Aug 15, 1941 Twin Falls, Idaho
2. Rhea Dee   "   Born Feb. 6, 1943   "   "   "
3. Bethene O'Nole "   Born May 15, 1945   "   "   "

Nancy Blake Ketchum
Born: Jan 6, 1860 San Saba
Died Jan 9, 1937 Knickerbocker, Tex
Married Dec. 11, 1879 to:

Abigah Blum Duncan
Born: Nov. 20, 1856
Died June 27, 1915 Knickerbocker, Tex
Children:
1. Dilia Green Duncan - daughter - Lucille Son - Blake Born 1903 Nov.
   Blake, lived w/ Nancy + B. Lee
   Born Oct. 25, 1881 in San Saba County
   Died Nov. 25, 1915 buried in Knickerbocker.
2. Loyd Boy Duncan
   Lois Born Oct 5, 1883
   Died May 14, 1960 Lovelock, New
3. Cassandar Duncan
   Born Aug 2, 1885
   Died Aug 16, 1887 buried in Chrystoval, Tex
4. Jep Duncan
   Born Aug 6, 1887
   Died Feb 26, 1889 buried in Chrystoval, Tex
5. Berry Ketchum Duncan
   Born: Feb 19, 1889
   Died Dec 17, 1962 Buhl, Idaho
6. Ora Lee Duncan
   Born March 1, 1891 Knickerbocker
   Died Oct 11, 1966 Twin Falls, Idaho
7. Joe Carl Duncan
   Born Sept 1, 1893 Knickerbocker
   Died July 14, 1972 Kingman, Ariz
8. Gus Thomas Duncan
   Born Sept. 11, 1895 Knickerbocker
   Died May 31, 1955 Lovelock, New

Dear family and friends

Chet's Reflections is taken from old journals and writings of Chet Brackett. They are only as accurate as his memories. There are many more stories included in the journals. Surely there are different viewpoints from people with different perspectives. Two other books that are in the works, one on more Brackett family perspectives, one on three creek families and history. Any information on either is eagerly looked for. If you don't put for your perspective to us, we will still write the books using the information we have at hand. Please help us get as much information as accurate as possible. Any information you provide, that we don't have at hand will be sourced as coming from you. There are many good stories and information out there, please help us gather and share as much as possible.

Email to Chetbrack@gmail

or mail to:
    Chet Brackett
    HC 33 Box 111
    Rogerson, Idaho 83302

call Chet Brackett **208-731-0135**   or Kim Brackett **208-731-1037**

98070915R00092

Made in the USA
Lexington, KY
03 September 2018